Colin Townsend was born in Wimbledon SW19 but spent most of his upbringing in Norbury and Streatham. He completed an engineering apprenticeship. He then moved to Basingstoke for home and job, where he worked as an engineer for 40 years. He has a son and daughter and two grandchildren. His partner Sally passed away a few years ago; he is now retired and leads a group of walkers in the New Forest on behalf of Healthy Walks.

I would like to dedicate this book to my son Elliott and daughter Sarah, I am immensely proud of both of them.

Colin Townsend

# A COMMON MURDER

AUSTIN MACAULEY PUBLISHERS™

LONDON • CAMBRIDGE • NEW YORK • SHARJAH

A CIP catalogue record for this title is available from the British Library.

ISBN 9781035838776 (Paperback)
ISBN 9781035838783 (ePub e-book)

www.austinmacauley.co.uk

First Published 2024
Austin Macauley Publishers Ltd®
1 Canada Square
Canary Wharf
London
E14 5AA

# Chapter 1

James woke from a deep sleep; the alarm on his phone ringing loudly on the bedside cabinet. He had put it as usual in an old ashtray so that it made a bit more noise, otherwise, he could sleep all day. He got out of bed and showered quickly, it only took him seven minutes. As he was made to do after PE at school, he cleaned his teeth, which took about as long, but he liked to keep his teeth healthy. He went downstairs and was greeted straight away by his two Labradors, Porgy and Bess. The dogs weren't allowed upstairs and the only time they were, was when he put them in the bath which they did not like at all. It meant that he had to drag them by their leads. He couldn't understand that as at the first sign of water outdoors, they were galloping to get in. They were both golden Labradors and were sisters; he had decided on having two as he had heard that having one was a problem as they did not like being left on their own; they were fine together but one could wreck the place. He made some tea and had a bowl of cereal, then got ready for work. As soon as he went to put his shoes on, the dogs got very excited as usual, they knew that this meant going for a walk; it was still early.

Checking the time, it was 5 am, so he was on time. He liked to give the dogs a good walk before work. He didn't need to leave for work till 5:45, so he had time to let the labs get rid of some energy. He picked up their leads, and as soon as he did this, they whirled round in circles such was their delight. He locked the door behind him and crossed the road. The dogs sat at the edge of the road and kept to heal whilst walking in the street. He led them through an alley which led to another road which in turn led to the common. He waved the dogs off and they tore across the grass playing with each other. They were only 200 metres or so in when Porgy did her business and ran off ahead, quickly followed by Bess doing hers. James pulled out a plastic bag and scooped the poop in and tied it up; he would get rid of it in the bin provided at the edge of the common later. It was a job he disliked intently but understood that keeping places clean was a necessity.

Some way on and all was dark, the light from streetlights didn't carry this far and he could look up. It was a clear night and he loved looking up at the stars, there were hundreds of them. He knew the plough and found it easily but there was so much more to see. It was lucky that this path which cut this part of the common in half was flat with no stones, so he didn't have to worry about tripping. He walked his normal route straight across the common and back again, it wasn't until he turned around to walk back that he missed the dogs, he had been lost in thought of what he was doing at work as well as the night sky. He gave them a whistle, but that didn't work so he called their names… Porgy, Bess, Porgy, Bess. He took his torch out of his pocket and flashed it about, but no sign.

The only place they could be hidden from view was in the wooded area to his left. He called again; this time he heard a whine, and it came from the wooded area, he hoped to God that neither dog had got itself injured and tangled up amongst the brambles. Vet bills were costly. On getting to the edge of the wood, he could make out the dogs sitting among them; their being golden labs enabled James to see them. It was obvious that neither dog could not or would not come to him, so concerned, he went through some of the bushes and trees to find the dogs sitting by a large sack or something; then he realised it was a body.

The scene took the breath out of him; he couldn't think for a second what had happened, his eyes became accustomed to the light of his torch in the darkness then realised that it was the body of a girl, and she was only partially clothed. He went closer to see if there was any sign of life, but her eyes were open and she was so still and white. He wasn't sure what he should do, but he went closer and tried to feel for a pulse but couldn't get anything. He wasn't sure that he was doing it right, but she was cold as ice. He reached into his pocket for his mobile phone, realising that he had left it in the house. He put the dogs on their leads, petted them and told them that they were good dogs and led them out of the woods as quickly as possible. He turned back and said quietly to the girl laying there.

"I've got to leave you now, but I will be back with help, I promise."

He walked quickly to the house to retrieve his phone.

He dialled 999 on his phone, and the operator asked him what service he wanted, police, ambulance or fire brigade. He paused for a minute as he wasn't sure whether to ask for an ambulance as well; he knew that he needed police. He was sure she was dead but not absolutely, so he opted for the police as if they arrived quickly, they could get an ambulance if they found she was still alive.

He was put through to a police operator, who first took his name and address and then asked him the nature of his call. He explained that he had found a body on the common and said, "I tried for a pulse but found none, her eyes were open, and she was cold but I'm not one hundred per cent sure that she is dead. I think so but I'm not sure."

"Ok, sir, the police will be with you as soon as possible. Are you still at the scene?" He explained that the body was on the common.

"I will show the police as soon as they get here."

The operator called for an ambulance to attend as well in case she was alive.

The police were fast to respond and arrived in ten minutes. Whilst he waited, he went indoors and shut the dogs in the kitchen. Two police officers arrived in their car, and he went out to meet them. The ambulance arrived with lights flashing as well.

They got out of the vehicle with a large bag and joined the police and James.

"Evening, sir, you rang to report finding a body."

"Yes, on the common, I'm not completely sure that she is dead. Could we go straight away to find her?"

He locked the front door.

"You can't get your car or ambulance onto the common from here, you need to drive right round to the other side, but we can walk to where she is from here quickly."

"Ok, let's get there on foot and worry about the car and ambulance later, so lead on."

They walked across the common to where the woods started, they all had torches to see. James led them into the woods and shone his torch on the scrub ahead where the body was. The police officers saw her and could see quickly that there was no sign of life. The paramedics went closer to check and agreed. They asked James to stay back and one of them used his radio to call it in.

"Right, sir, I need to get the car over here, but I also need some details from you, so we need to get back to the car."

One of the policemen walked back with him, whilst the other stood guard over the body. The paramedics also went back with him and left in the ambulance.

"Right, we need some details from you first so may I come in for a moment?"

"Yes, ok I badly need a cup of tea, would you like one?"

They went indoors, he opened the kitchen door where the dogs were and turned on the kettle. Porgy and Bess made a fuss of the policeman whilst James made the tea. They sat down, the policeman said no to the cuppa but waited until James had sat down with his, noting the handshake. The policeman took his details down and he explained how he had found the body, or rather how the dogs had found her, his hands were shaking badly now. "Did you touch her?"

"Yes," he said, "I checked or at least tried to check her pulse."

"Ok, you will have to give a statement and give us fingerprints and DNA at the station. Thank you for your call, we need to get this investigation started."

The policeman left to get the car across the common.

The police car drove around the roads passing between parts of the common until it could pull off of the road and drive across the grass to where the policeman who had waited by the body was signalling with his torch, the blue lights spinning around, lit up the common. He stopped the car five metres from the trees. Both men then walked to the boot and took out several rolls of blue and white tape with **POLICE LINE DO NOT CROSS** on them, they proceeded to tape off a large area of ground.

They had no sooner accomplished that, when more headlights and blue lights appeared across the common this was a van and behind it a car, the police doctor had arrived. He got out and put on a white paper suit, blue plastic shoes and rubber gloves. He ducked under the tape and carrying a torch in one hand and an instrument bag in the other, went to the body.

The doctor quickly examined her, pronounced her dead and took some temperatures so that he could work out the time of death. He moved some of the clothes on the top part of the body to see her head and face clearly. He ducked under the tape again and said to the sergeant who had arrived in the van.

"She died between 8 and 10 o'clock; looks like she's been killed with a blow or blows to the back of her head, so blunt force trauma will be the cause of death, but that is conjecture at this time, we will know more after the inquest you can carry on now."

The sergeant took some weighty bags out of the back of the van, the first thing was to give the girl some modesty; a heavy blanket was taken by two policemen and draped over the body. The other bag contained a large tent with poles which was put up over the body to keep the site pristine and keep onlookers from seeing anything. The sergeant and the other policeman returned to the station. The original officers were then tasked with guarding the scene.

James had managed to down another cup of tea and even managed to eat some toast before locking up; he rang work and told them that he wouldn't be in. He gave a cursory explanation but didn't want to say too much. He was sitting in his conservatory; it was bright and peaceful with both dogs curled around his ankles. The traumatic events of the morning fell heavily on him; he turned on the radio for some light morning chat and sat down and eventually fell into a deep sleep.

# Chapter 2

The sun rose at last over the scene; it was going to be a clear sunny day again. The two policemen looked around, they were on the edge of the common. The Hawthorn trees were predominant and the brambles were many and full of thorns and blackberries covering the area, the grass was short with all kinds of plants growing, Lady's slipper, orange and yellow, Harebells of pale blue and other plants, then there was a cinder path which stretched from an alleyway between two cemeteries to the main Croydon Road, then the scrub, mainly blackthorn and brambles with loads of thorns. Over the other side of the wild scrub were some council houses which led to the main road. To one end was a cemetery and on the other, more council houses. The policemen were happy to be going home soon, they had finished their shift; it was someone else's problem now.

Another police car arrived, and two officers got out they said their hellos to the sentries and took over that duty.

*****************

The phone rang, waking her up from a deep sleep. Detective Inspector Jean Hardy answered tiredly, "Hello."

That was all she could manage to say being woken up in the middle of the night. "What is it?"

"Sorry to bother you, ma'am, but we have a suspicious death on Mitcham Common. Reports are that it is a young female, but I have no more details."

"Okay, will be at the station as soon as I can."

She looked at the time; it was 6.10 am and still dark. She lay back for a moment to wake up properly and get her thoughts together. She got up, showered then dressed. Her bedroom was plainly painted in a neutral yellow colour with colourful pictures and light oak furniture.

The bedspread was also colourful matching the pictures and covering a double bed. She was a divorcee and that being an amicable arrangement with her ex, John who was still about and they met every now and then for a drink and dinner, neither of them had another partner at present, they had just fallen out of love. Their jobs could have been part of the problem as he was a doctor, so neither of them had 9 to 5 jobs, so saw each other when they could, even holidays were a problem as both had to arrange cover.

She went downstairs and made breakfast-muesli and toast with marmalade. She put her shoes on and went out to her car. She drove a Mini as she didn't do many miles, at least in her own car, and drove to Croydon Police Station. She parked around the back and went inside and up to her office on the second floor. The police station itself was old but had been completely renovated inside with modern furniture; she sat down and was given a mug of coffee and read the reports of the evening and looking at the details of the suspicious death, All there was had been the script of what was said on the phone by the person who found the body and details about him. She called for a car and Sergeant Walters took some keys off a board and walked over.

"Ready when you are, boss," he said.

"Right bring Isabel with you, meaning Isabel Johnstone, the detective, constable and let's go."

Jean Hardy was 5 feet 10 inches tall and was a little overweight, she had blonde hair and blue eyes and wore a minimum of face paint, lipstick, and mascara, and that was it. She wore a necklace of silver and matching earrings. She liked to have a minimum of bureaucracy, so they all got on well in the office and she only used rank when out of the station.

They drove though the traffic along the main road. They didn't get held up and although they hadn't used their blue lights, the police car was given respect from motorists, and turned off onto the common. They drove across the common to the scene of crime they could see that there was already plenty of activity there. As they arrived, the Scene of Crime Officers (SOCO's) forensic team also drove up. They got out of the car and approached the blue tape; Jean nodded hello to the policeman on guard duty.

She ducked under the tape with Sergeant John Walters and Detective Constable Isabel Johnstone in close pursuit and all three putting on white suits with gloves and booties went to look at the body. One of the forensic teams took the blanket off of the body. They took the scene in; then the forensics were waiting to do their jobs, so they left everything to them. To let them get on with their jobs, they left without causing any interference. She just muttered to the forensic team to deal with her body first, and get her away to the mortuary to give her some dignity.

"Naturally," they said. "Of course, we will."

# Chapter 3

Jean Hardy said to them all that it looked as if the body had just been dumped there and the crime had been committed elsewhere. There were drag marks visible, but they should know more after the inquest and after forensics have taken a look. "Sergeant, please see to it that the cemetery is searched as well. We need to find her missing clothing and maybe that could be where she died." They went back to the car and to the station. Jean got the troops together then went to a large whiteboard that dominated the room and wrote on it 'Murder on the common.'

She made a list.

Name and address

Time of death **8–10 0'clock**

Cause of death

Where did she die?

**How did she get there?**

Friends and relatives

Suspects

She then addressed the waiting officers, "Right, there has been a murder committed on Mitcham Common. We don't have many details yet, but we need to start getting together what we do know, we do have an approximate time of death."

"We are looking at a sexual crime though this has yet to be confirmed yet; for our purpose, we will assume it is, so we will make a list of possible people who have convictions for this or similar crimes. Our main point to be found asap is her identification; she looked to be fairly young, so I would have expected her to be in possession of a bag and or telephone which has yet to be discovered. Dick will give you your independent workload."

Sergeant Dick Walters gave out the jobs to all by 11:00 am; there was a list of previous offenders from the computer to sort through.

Meanwhile, at the site of the murder, policemen were scouring the area with fingertips in some places and raking through the ditches; this brought anything in them to the surface and out of the stagnant water, apart from old bicycle wheels and tyres and other rubbish came their first find and the most important so far, the shoulder bag of the girl, it was bagged up immediately and the forensic people took it. One of them immediately rushed it to the lab where it could be examined properly.

The outside was examined first to see if there were any fingerprints, or DNA such as blood or saliva although there was not much of a chance of that, considering where it was found, but it was procedure.

The bag was carefully opened and a wallet containing bank cards in it was found; from this, they attained her name and address. The rest of the contents of her bag were checked out. There was the normal make-up as well as a bunch of keys which after forensic examination could be used to get into her house, as one of them was a Yale type of door key.

Jane walked to the whiteboard and rubbed out the name and address and put her name and address up.

### Jennifer Harrow, 25 Branksome Avenue, Mitcham

Jean called over to David to go with her to first pick up the set of keys and then on to the property.

They arrived outside her house and parked behind a small Citroen. Nigel pressed a fob which was attached to the keys, and the lights flashed, so this was her car. He re-locked it and called back to the office to have the car removed and ready for examination. He then joined Jane and they rang the front doorbell in case there was someone in. There was no one in, so they tried a Yale key from the ones they had found into the lock of the front door; it fit and the door opened.

They got dressed in white paper suits and plastic overshoes and rubber gloves and went in. Inside, they found a fairly nice sized lounge which had painted walls in an off-white pink colour, a small TV, and a pink suite comprising of a two-seater settee and matching chair. Next to that room was a bedroom with painted walls, double bed with bedside cabinets, and some photos on the wall of presumably family. The bathroom was off this room. They checked the bathroom cabinets and after a quick check of them, found nothing other than make-up remover, spare toothbrush and paste; other clinical necessities, nothing unusual. The kitchen was clean and tidy. They started methodically searching, if they found anything they wanted to look more closely at, they bagged it up and placed it in the hall for removal. They left with a laptop computer, a diary and a photograph of her.

They locked up the flat and went back to the office.

"Right, David. I'll take a look at the diary, and you look at the PC and put the photograph on the whiteboard so we can all see it," said Jean. Then they asked SOCO to look at the house and car.

By the end of the day at 5:00 pm, the police were in possession of the contact details from her laptop computer; there were pictures as well.

One of the staff checked for social media, but she did not use it.

# Chapter 4

As a result of everything, they looked at what they had on the whiteboard although it was still being updated.

Jane called everyone together in the office.

"Right," she said, "let's look at what we have already. Our victim's name is Jennifer Harrow. She lived at 25 Branksome Avenue, Mitcham. She is 20 years old."

"She was an attractive girl, as you can see from the picture The time of death is still between 8 and 10 o'clock. We need to get the murderer as quickly as possible as they could decide to kill again, especially as this looks to be a sexually-motivated murder. According to the post-mortem, she was bludgeoned to death. Although her lower clothing was partially removed, there was no sign of penetration; considering the crime, this is surprising. So, we need to look at the offender, possibly being a female as well as a male."

"There were no fingerprints on her or her handbag except for hers. There was no DNA other than hers. We await any findings from her flat or car."

"We need to find her relatives and see if there were any she was particularly close to. Let's see her contact list, and look for friends at her place of work, we need to get a list of suspects. We also need to find her clothes as they may well be in the place where she was killed. There is missing jewellery, so we need to find that. There were marks on her neck showing that she was wearing a necklace of some kind and it had left signs of being ripped off."

"Right, let's get on. I know everything is vague but hopefully, things will become clearer, as we get answers from SOCO."

It didn't take too long to find Jennifer's relatives' names and addresses in her diary. Jennifer's mother lived not too far away, in Basingstoke about 50 miles away, so Jean liaised with the police there to let her mother know what had happened.

Two policemen or rather one policeman and one policewoman called around as soon as they could; the door was opened by a woman of about 50 years old, she was about 5 feet 5 inches tall with grey hair, a pinched nose, well dressed, with a cat in her arms.

They asked if they were talking to Nancy Harrow. "Yes," she said.

"Are you the mother of Jennifer Harrow living at 25 Branksome Avenue Mitcham?"

"Yes," she said trembling now.

They sat her down then tactfully as possible told her what had happened, that her daughter had been found dead, but gave no other details. It was no surprise that she fell apart; they stayed with her for about an hour and on asking, they phoned a friend for her, who hurried across to comfort her. Both officers were glad to get away from the house.

"Glad to get away from there, I hate this sort of thing, but I know it has to be done," said the policewoman.

Her colleague agreed.

# Chapter 5

The police in Croydon worked into the evening and from the information gathered from the diary and laptop, it was showing that her main hobby was walking. Her friends were listed. She had only started her job five weeks ago and had no special friends or boyfriends there. She was friendly with everyone, but no one really knew her personally, they had a list of her main friends.

**Sarah Haliday**
**Jennifer Jordan**
**Adrian Hewitt**
**David Johnston**
**Paul Houlton**
**Sally Parsons**

David Walters gave out each name for the detective constables to do checks and find out about, including interviews and statements.

DC Pertwee checked out Sarah Halliday. He first checked social media where he found her as a bright spark and dancing the nights away. She was pretty, dressed up for a party where there were pictures of her with her partner. She was about 5 feet 5 inches tall, with mousy hair in a modern bob, very curvy and looked very fit. There was no fat on her body. She enjoyed outdoor activities and dancing with her partner, Jonathon Davies and seemed pretty tight with him. He was taller by a few inches and was with her outdoors and dancing in her pictures. He looked to have a bit of excess weight on him, but not much. He was an accountant working in the city whilst she was a secretary with an engineering company.

He found her address which was in a newly-built estate near Hook and went round to see her in the evening allowing time for her to get home from work. The pair lived in a new or possibly a couple of years old two-bedroom house. It was one of those houses that looked slim and in a small block but was like a Tardis looking bigger on the inside. She answered the door and was shocked to see a police warrant card and let him in. She was shocked to hear of Jennifer's death. She hadn't seen her for a while, was an old school friend but met her for a coffee occasionally, but as she lived a fair way from her, they didn't meet often, but they all went on walks. She didn't know if Jennifer had a boyfriend but was able to give an alibi that she and her boyfriend Jonathan were at the house all evening together.

"Was there anyone else at the flat that could verify the alibi?" He asked.

"No," she said.

She couldn't think of anyone who had feelings for Jennifer good or bad, off-hand.

He asked that she attend the station to give a formal statement, as they had to make everything official. He asked her whether she would mind if they took fingerprints and DNA, but that they would be destroyed as soon as the investigation was finished. He also told her he needed to interrogate her mobile phone but she could have it back fairly quickly. She said that she would attend the next afternoon. He asked also for her partner to do the same. She said that it shouldn't be a problem. He gave her his card and said to ask for him at the station.

DC Janice Harwell was checking up on Jenifer Jordan. She was also on social media, an avid walker and had walked with Jennifer and the others a few weeks ago. She was a bubbly blonde with a sturdy figure. She stood about 5 feet 6 inches and lived in an upstairs flat in a two-storey block of flats.

It was evening that Janice called on her. She was working at a department store in town where she was the manager of the lighting section. On the night in question, she had been down at a pub, the Horse and Groom with other friends. She also didn't know whether Jennifer had a boyfriend but was sure that she must have. She listed the friends she was down the pub with, and when asked about the people on their list, she spoke nicely of them. They all enjoyed walking in the countryside. She was quite upset to hear that Jennifer had lost her life although Janice didn't tell her how she had died. Janice also asked her to attend the police station for a formal statement and give fingerprints and DNA. She knew anyone with feelings for Jennifer good or bad, she couldn't think of anyone having feeling for or against her, but if she thought of someone, she would let them know. Janice gave her a card with her details on it and left, leaving her upset with the death of Jennifer.

DC John Waiter called on Adrian Hewitt who was surprised to get a visit from the police and was very upset to hear about Jennifer. He lived in a single room within a large house. He was aged about 20 and was 6 feet 1 inch tall with thickset black hair. He had a rugged face and his nose had been broken at some point; it didn't disfigure him but made him appear more interesting. DC Waiter made a note of it as it could possibly show violent tendencies and they could use that in the interview, and he had seen Jennifer the week before when he and Jennifer walked alone, as the others couldn't make it that week. They had been texting each other about the next walk. His alibi was that he was at home on his own, so no alibi in reality. He was also asked to attend the police station for a formal statement and asked if he had any objection to them taking fingerprints and DNA, He said he had no problem with that. He was also asked if he knew of anyone who had feelings good or bad for Jennifer. DC John Waiter thought that more questions needed asking but that under oath would be better. He asked him to attend the station for a formal statement plus have his fingerprint and DNA taken. He explained that it was just a procedure and not to worry.

DC Roger Bailey visited David Johnstone who was equally shocked to get a visit from the police and was also upset to hear of Jennifer's demise; also a walker he did not know if Jennifer had a boyfriend and had been working in Newcastle, well not working at that time, but was in the bar with other people attending the course that he was on. He had only got back that morning. The alibi was going to be substantiated, but nevertheless, he asked Roger to attend the station for a formal statement.

David Johnston visited the police station for his interview. He asked for Roger Bailey at the desk and was shown to an interview room where he was joined by DC Bailey and Niall Glover who turned on the tape machine and said for the tape, the date and time, then who was in the room.

He asked for David's date of birth, address, and phone number then he was asked whether he had ever been in Jennifer's house, or if she had been in his.

"No," he said.

"Have you ever been out with her?"

"No, I have a steady girlfriend."

"Has she ever mentioned a partner to you?"

"No," he said.

"Can you tell me where you were that day and night, please?"

"Yes, I was in Newcastle on a course for work. In the evening, I was in the bar chatting to some of the other guests, they will remember me. I went to bed at about 1:00 am."

"Thank you, now all we need are your fingerprints, DNA and access to your phone then you can go."

DC Niall Glover went to visit Paul Houlton who wasn't surprised to be interviewed, he was still shocked from hearing of Jennifer's death from one of the walkers. It was David Johnston who had rung him. He was another walker but hadn't been for a while as he had broken an ankle playing football. He didn't have an alibi but was walking on crutches. He didn't know of any boyfriend but was sure that if she had one, he would be a walker. He didn't know of anyone she had come up against and would attend the station for an interview and statement.

DC Janet Dores visited Sally Parsons; she was also upset; she had seen Jennifer go out to watch a film and have coffee afterwards a couple of days before. They had chatted and she had said that she had recently seen someone that she didn't like at all, and was very surprised to see, but she wasn't completely sure that it was who she had at first thought it was. She had indicated that Sally knew him too. She also had an alibi as she was working behind the bar at a local pub, the Pollard Oak. He asked her to think about things and explained they needed to find out if she had any boyfriends or whether she could think about whether Jennifer had given any clue as to who it was that she didn't like. He gave her his card and asked that she attend the station for a formal statement and fingerprints, DNA, and check her mobile phone. He thanked her and left.

# Chapter 6

The forensic report and the autopsy report were now available, and Jean called all her staff together to review the documents and the visits to friends and relatives of Jennifer.

Jean took the reports which were also projected on a large screen. "Right, let's look again at the facts. Her name was Jennifer Harrow, living at 25 Branksome Avenue, Mitcham. She was murdered by blunt force trauma but where her body was found on Mitcham Common was not where she was killed; she was partially clothed. She was dressed above the waist but naked below but appeared to be unmolested. Her bag with belongings was found nearby in a ditch. There was a set of keys which we found to be for her car and front door. She lived in a downstairs flat which was clean and tidy. Forensics are going through it at present. The cemetery was searched but so far, there has been no sign of her missing clothing or belongings. Her mother has been informed and it appears that she had no other relatives. Right," said Jean, "where are we with regard to friends?"

DC Janice Harwell spoke. "I checked on Jenifer Jordan, she was upset at the news and hadn't seen Jennifer for a couple of weeks but knew nothing and had an alibi."

DC John Waiter reported on Adrian Hewitt. "The same with him; was upset to hear of her death, but he saw her a week ago and had texted her about walks during the week. He lives on his own, is about 20 and had no alibi. He also has a broken nose, which could possibly be a pointer to violent behaviour. There is nothing from Criminal Records Office (CRO) on him. He has no alibi."

DC Roger Bailey said that David Johnstone had not seen her for a while and had an alibi.

DC Niall Glover said Paul Houlton hadn't seen her for a few weeks and had a broken leg and was on crutches.

DC Janet Dores spoke up about Sally Parsons. "She had been out with Jennifer two days before her death. They had been to see a film and went for a coffee; she said that Jennifer had seen someone recently that she didn't like at all but she wouldn't say who it was other than it would come as a surprise to Sally, and if it was who she thought it was then Sally knew him too. She had an alibi and was working, but could be worth interrogating further about the person she didn't like as maybe we could jog her memory as to who it might be."

"Let's interview Sally Parsons to see if we can get anything else from her by jogging her memory regarding this person she disliked, but give her some time to dwell on it. That's a good line of enquiry. Adrian Hewitt hasn't got an alibi, so let's get him in as well and let's look at him in detail."

Two days later, Paul Hewton hobbled into the station on crutches and asked for Niall Glover. He was shown to an interview room where he was met by DC Glover and DC Roger Bailey who turned on the tape machine.

He gave his name, address and phone number.

"Thank you for making the effort to come in sir, we'll be as brief as possible. We know that you have an alibi due to your broken ankle. What we need to know is whether you ever went to her house or whether she ever visited yours?"

"No, can't say she did."

"Was there any familiarity between you and Jennifer?"

"Well, no but I did ask her out once, but she refused."

"Did you keep trying?"

"No, not really, I didn't, she made it quite plain that to keep on would damage our friendship."

"Well, thank you, sir, if you would just be good enough to give us your fingerprints and DNA sample and let us access your mobile phone then you can go. We'll see about getting you a lift home considering your condition."

"Thanks," he said.

# Chapter 7

Adrian Hewitt was next to arrive and was shown to an interview room.

Two detectives came into the room and sat down opposite Adrian. David Walters turned on the tape-recording machine. Inspector Jean Hardy said for the tape that she was Inspector Hardy and accompanying her was Sergeant David Walters, she then said the date and looking at her watch, the time and that they were interviewing Adrian Hewitt, "Right," she said, "can you give me your date of birth?"

He answered that one.

"Your address?"

"34, Hawthorne Road, Thornton Heath," he said.

"Where were you born?"

"London," he replied.

"Whereabouts in London, please?"

"I don't know," he muttered.

She looked at him intently for a moment.

"Ok, we'll come back to that, where did you go to school?"

"Gonville School as an infant and then Norbury Manor."

"Ok," she said, "where do you work?"

"A & C Harris," he said, "Commonside East, Mitcham. I work as an engineer fitter there."

"What is your relationship with Jennifer Harrow"?

"I walk in the countryside with her and count her as a friend."

"How long have you been walking with her?"

"About three years now."

"Have you ever been to her home?"

"Yes, a few times."

"When was the last time you visited her?"

"About a week or two ago."

"Has she ever visited you?"

"Yes, once last week, she called and took me by surprise, I am not that untidy, but my place is only a room and is a bit cluttered."

"Have you ever been romantically involved with her?"

"No, we are just good friends, that's all."

"Has she told you of a boyfriend or someone she didn't like at all?"

"No."

"Is there anyone that you know of that could be going out with her?"

"No."

"Right, Mr Hewitt, can you give me your whereabouts from 8:00 pm to 4:00 am on the night in question? Please be specific, we need to know exactly, if you went down to the shops for a snack or something, we need to know. Now is your chance to tell me something that you haven't already said."

"Got home about 6:00 pm and was indoors watching telly, planning a route for hiking until about 11:00 pm, then went to bed, woke up about 6:30 am."

"How did you get your broken nose?"

"Hit it with a spanner; it was a large spanner and quite high up and it wasn't the right spanner and slipped off a bolt and caught me a good one."

"Are you sure that you didn't get it fighting?"

"Positive."

"Have you any pictures of Jennifer?"

"Yes, on my phone when we were walking."

"Okay, Mr Hewitt, as soon as you have given us your fingerprints and DNA and mobile phone, you can go."

He handed over his phone.

"When can I have my phone back, I use it all the time and as an alarm clock."

"You can collect it in a couple of hours."

He went out of the station after they took his prints and his DNA. He walked around Croydon for a while then sought out a coffee shop, sat down with a Latte and thought about his experience and about Jennifer which was very upsetting, but he couldn't think about that at the present as he felt that he was in danger as they had made it plain that he was a suspect. Did they really think that he was responsible? For god's sake, he wouldn't hurt a fly, maybe it was just his imagination, perhaps this was just the way they did their investigation processes. No matter, it still made him feel guilty, but oh hell, he didn't know. He couldn't go home for a while as they had his mobile phone, and he needed that back.

After a couple of hours, he went back to the station and picked up his phone, then caught the bus home.

# Chapter 8

Sally Parsons arrived at the station, and asked for DC Janet Dores who took her to the interview room and explained that statements were made on tape nowadays, she turned on the tape recorder and said that this was an interview with Sally Parsons in attendance.

Inspector Jean Hardy spoke her name and Detective Constable Janet Dores spoke her name.

"Hello, Sally," said Janet, "this is an interview to formalise what you have spoken to DC Dores about."

"Full name, please."

"Sally Helen Parsons."

"Can you give me your date of birth?"

She answered.

"Your address?"

"21 fortress Lane Hackbridge."

"Where were you born?"

"Basingstoke," she replied.

"Where did you go to school?"

"Fairfield School as an infant and then at John Hunt of Everest."

"Where do you work?"

"The Pollard Oak Pub in Mitcham. I work as a bar maid there. whilst I am looking for a new job."

"What is your relationship with Jennifer Harrow?"

"I walk in the countryside with her, and we've been friends for years. I went to school with her at Everest and came up to get a job with better prospects and money. I got a job as a secretary working at Mallards in Hackbridge but they folded up, so I work at the pub till I get something else."

"Have you ever been to her home?"

"Yes, a few times."

"When was the last time you visited her?"

"About three weeks ago."

"Has she ever visited you?"

"Yes, a couple of times, we saw a film and had coffee three days before, you know, she passed."

"Has she told you of her boyfriend?"

"No."

"You mentioned that she had seen or met someone she didn't like and whose identity would surprise you."

"As asked, I've wracked my brains and can't think who it could be."

"Do you think it could be one of the walkers?"

"No, she said that I knew him too."

"Right, Sally, give me your whereabouts from 8:00 pm to 4:00 am on the night in question, we need to know exactly if you went down the shops for some food or something, we need to know. Now is your chance to tell me something that you haven't already said."

"I started work at 6 o'clock and I finished at midnight; after clearing up, went to bed and slept through the night."

"Have you any pictures of Jennifer?"

"Yes, on my phone."

"We would like to check your mobile phone with your permission and password; you can have it back in a few hours."

"Okay."

"Okay, Sally, as soon as you have given us your fingerprints and DNA, you can go."

"Can you keep thinking if there is someone that was upsetting Jennifer and let us know if you think of anyone?"

Sarah Haliday arrived for her interview with her partner Johnathon Davies; they were separated, then shown into separate interview rooms; two pairs of detectives went in to interview them.

They were each interviewed on tape with the detectives introducing themselves and asking the questions that needed answering.

The main question was where they were during the critical hours, whether they were together, whether they had been to her house or her to theirs. They asked Jonathon if he had ever been out with Jennifer or tried to see her, to which he replied that he hadn't. They told him that anything he said was confidential and wouldn't be told to Sarah, but he maintained that he hadn't been in her house or been out with Jennifer.

After submitting to finger printing and DNA collection, they were asked for their mobile phones, and then let go.

Jennifer Jordan arrived at the station and asked for Janice Harwell. Janice came down to the front desk and showed her up to one of the interview rooms.

"Thanks for coming," she said.

She was joined by Roger Walters who turned on the tape machine, and after stating the time and date introduced them all on tape.

"Can we have your date of birth and address please?"

"Phone number home and mobile please?"

She gave them the answers.

"How long have you known Jennifer?"

"About six months."

"How did you meet?"

"I joined the hiking group; I'd heard about them from another friend David Johnson. I love to walk in the country so joined up. It's not a club with a subscription, and that also appealed to me. It's been good, but I'm not sure it will be good in the future after this."

"I suppose that Adrian will possibly carry it on, he is the leader and talks about the history in the areas we walked in, and the wild life around that we might see, mind you we never see much as we make too much noise."

"Do you know of Jennifer's private life, whether she had a boyfriend or whatever?"

"No, not really, we chatted as you do when walking and when we stopped for lunch but just chatter, we didn't chat about that sort of thing."

"Ok, give me your whereabouts for the day of Jennifer's death?"

"I was in London working in Blackfriars as a receptionist at WK Denims where I work, then got home about 8:00 pm watched the telly and went to bed."

"Was there anyone with you?"

"No, I was alone."

"Have you ever been in Jennifer's house, or has she been to yours?"

"No, never," she said.

"Ok, thank you, would you leave us your mobile phone if you unlock it, we can change it so that it stays open, and also, we need your fingerprints and a sample of DNA, then you can go, we will be finished with your phone in about two hours if you want to collect it."

# Chapter 9

"Well, it doesn't look as if we have many suspects, we need to see who else she was friendly with. There must be many more than we have listed. Come on, people, we need more names. We know that she enjoyed walking, but what else did she like to do in her spare time? We need to interview her mother properly to find out from her about her daughter. See what she did at school, where she went to school, if she had any boyfriends or who her girlfriends were, let's get to it, and interview her at home, I want to do that myself."

Jean was driven to Basingstoke by Sergeant Walters. The door was answered by a tearful Nancy Harrow.

"Hello, Mrs Harrow, you have my commiserations on your daughter. We need for you to come over to Croydon and give a formal identification, I am terribly sorry to bother you at this time, but we need to find out all we can about Jennifer."

"Where she went to school; who her friends were at school and enemies as well if you know of any, and boyfriends and would-be boyfriends, you know anyone who liked her, but she did not like them. Could we see where she stayed when she was down here, please?" Nancy showed them upstairs to Jennifer's room. They looked around the room where Jennifer had lived. There were the normal pictures, awards, and teddy bears, Nancy talked about her daughter's achievements. She had medals for competing in gymnastics when she was ten years old, but with age came the learning to get good grades and she had given it up.

"I apologise in advance if we are asking questions that you have already been asked before," said Jean.

"We are looking for someone in connection to her death as we are treating this as a murder."

"How was she killed?"

"She was found with blunt force trauma."

"Sorry, what does that mean?"

"She was hit over the head with something."

"Oh God, was she raped as well?"

"No."

Jean paused for her to let that all sink in.

"Right, we have it that Jennifer was born in Basingstoke, went to Fairfield's Primary School, then on to John Hunt of Everest, did she go elsewhere after John Hunt?"

"Yes, she went to Basingstoke College and studied English as she wanted to be a secretary. She got her qualifications and looked for a job. There was nothing in Basingstoke, so she tried adverts in papers and found the job that she had recently left. She had her digs then, so looked for something in that area, and recently started a new job there."

"What about friends, boyfriends in particular?"

"She had work friends, but not to meet socially. She had no boyfriend lately. If there was someone on the scene, she didn't say anything about him. But she didn't say anything about her private life, she kept that to herself."

Jean thanked her and then left. Nancy mentioned that she had a boyfriend whilst at school but thought it had fizzled out well before college.

On the drive home, Jean thought about the progress if any that they had made. They had the makings of a list of suspects; she knew there was plenty to do but she needed all the facts from the post-mortem and the forensic investigation.

She asked Sergeant Walters to go to the post-mortem and report back with details as soon as possible. The area search was underway and that was still in the hand of uniform, so they just had to wait for details.

DC Isabel Johnston went to Basingstoke Police Station and asked for help in locating the old school friends and where they were now. Jean had sent her to find out what she could. It didn't take too long to trace them using the electoral roll, DVLA to find out whether they had driving licences and where they lived, so Isabel was soon at their houses and knocking on their doors. They had not heard that Jennifer was dead, both of the women she talked to had good alibis, and when questioned about boyfriends knew very little other than she had had one. There had been a boy that she had met to go to school with but neither girl could remember his name and she had lost contact with them outside of school, so they had assumed that she had been with him.

The friend was someone that they would like to meet, but there was no sign of him, so she left for home without a name but knowing that he existed. However, this was whilst she was at school, and she would have been 16, so may well be of no consequence.

Two days later, Jennifer's mother arrived in Croydon by train with the friend who had stayed with her since she had been told of her daughter's death; transport had been arranged to get to and from the morgue. She was taken to a room with a curtained window in it; a woman came out and explained that the curtains would be opened and she would then view the body which would be covered from the chin down.

"Will I not be able to say goodbye properly to her, to touch her and give her a kiss."

"I'm sorry, but when Jennifer is taken by the undertakers then you will be able to say your goodbyes. Are you ready?"

"Yes, as ready as I will ever be."

She led them over to the curtain and then opened it.

Although her mother was expecting it, it still came as a shock to see her daughter laying there. She just managed a yes, that's her before she broke down. You expected your children to bury you, not for a parent to bury their child. Between the attendant and her friend, they managed to move her to another room which was furnished with a sofa and table and they gave both her mother and her friend a cup of tea with plenty of sugar.

They gave her some time to gather herself before she was taken to the railway station where she could get a train and go home.

# Chapter 10

At the morning briefing where the possible suspects were being investigated, it was decided that after alibis were checked, more investigation was needed. The police were running out of suspects; they had few leads, but it was early days yet.

A new day dawned, and Jean called the team together to review what they had; they had not very much evidence, but Adrian was the main person in the picture.

"Right," Jane called out, "I want some of you to concentrate on Adrian Harrow. I want to know where he went to school, what he was like at school, about his friends about his work, and who he hung out with there. What he does in his spare time? I want to know anything and everything about him."

This would take some time.

They discovered that he was an orphan who had been in a children's home for most of his life from birth to 16. He had been a quiet child and had mainly chosen to keep to himself. Most children from this home ended up in the armed forces but he had managed to get accepted as a trainee at a company manufacturing conveyor and lift systems. He seemed to have fitted in there quite well. He had been in trouble a bit at school, he started at second school ok but was of the sort that got bullied. He backed down from fights. Then when he was 15; it all changed; one particular boy, who bullied him started on him with his fists, and waited for him after school full of confidence with many others who wanted to watch, but at this point, Adrian had mentally had enough and he rebelled against the choice of running away. It was a long walk down from the school entrance to the gates where the crowd awaited him. As soon as he reached the gates, he was surrounded and bustled but he didn't wait to be hit first; he just went for it. He seemed to suddenly change and knocked the other boy for six hitting him again and again in rapid succession till he couldn't stand up; the other boy had not been able to lay a punch on him and after that, if anyone went for him, he was ready for them, and reacted quickly and violently. He was a changed boy, but he didn't become a callous attacker. He only went after boys who went for him.

He had become interested in nature and that led to hiking through the countryside and woods and that was his hobby now. Most of the people who asked about him agreed he was a genuinely good individual, and hiking had become his favourite hobby and he was dedicated to leading the group of hikers, although it wasn't a club as such it brought him joy and kept him fit.

He lived in one room in a large house, so not yet on the property ladder. His other hobby was football; he loved playing, but they wouldn't let him at school. They wanted him to play rugby. He supported Crystal Palace and went to watch them but was not part of the violent element.

"Right," Jane Hardy said, "let's get him back in."

Andrew was asked to come back in. Jean wanted to put some pressure on him whilst he was there. He arrived there the next evening because of work and was shown into one of the interview rooms. He found the room very intimidating. The walls were painted white with a large mirror on one wall, and the only furniture was a table and four chairs. A policeman stayed in the room, staying by the door, he feared that he would be lucky to get out, but he had done nothing wrong and hoped that he was wrong, The door opened and the two detectives entered the room, one of them started a tape recorder said the date and time then Inspector Jean Hardy and Sergeant David Walters asked if he would like a solicitor present.

"No," he said, "I haven't done anything wrong."

They asked him for his name, address, and date of birth, then asked him to give his detailed whereabouts that day, with times where possible. They asked him about his relationship with Jennifer and the last time they had been in contact, the last time they had been in physical contact, not by phone. They went over it with him and then asked if he knew of her boyfriend or anyone else that had any dealings with her.

"No," he said, "we didn't talk about things like that."

"What did you talk about?"

"The countryside, nature, things that were happening."

"What about her friends' relations or anything?"

He told them of the walkers, and who they were.

He told them where he went to school, how long he intended to stay in the room he lived in, how long he had known her, and places he had been with her. What was his relationship with her when was the last time he had seen her;

47

they went on and on, they were relentless. They were asking him questions he couldn't answer.

"We will give you a little time to think before we ask more questions of you." They took him down to the cells faced with a very heavy door with a peephole, to keep an eye on him. There was a hard bed at the end of the cell which went from one wall to the other; next was a toilet and a handbasin not very nice, they made him take off his shoes and belt and then locked him in. The door shut with a smooth click.

He felt claustrophobic and panicked a bit and was sweating.

He wondered briefly whether he needed to get a solicitor. No. He thought, why should he, he hadn't done anything wrong. He couldn't afford one anyway.

It was obvious to him that he was the main, and only suspect.

If they let him out, they would be keeping tabs on him and if they could find anything, they would get him in again and not let him out. He hoped that they would let him out soon, the room was so claustrophobic. He lounged on the bed and waited, planning in his head as to what he would do if he was ever let out.

# Chapter 11

Two hours later, he was escorted back to the interview room. The tape recorder was put back on.

"Right, Andrew, have you thought any more about things? Can we get you a solicitor to help you?"

"Yes, if you are paying but no if you're not."

"Let me ask you straight, did you kill her?"

"No, I did not," he replied.

"Look, I can understand if she wouldn't cooperate with your advances, we know you have a bit of a temper. Be straight with us come on."

"I am being straight with you."

"We wish to search your room. Do we need to get a warrant or will you let us?"

"Yes, search it all you want; you won't find anything incriminating."

"Right, let me explain what we are going to do next; you will be formally charged with murder, and we will bail you to return, you must give up your passport and report to the station every week," Jean said.

Adrian was panicking now but trying his best to conceal his anguish.

"I haven't got a passport."

"We can check on that."

"May I ask that you keep the investigation open because I am not the killer?" Adrian finalised.

They took him out to where a uniformed sergeant was sitting behind a large, elevated desk, then they uttered the words that chilled him.

"Adrian Hewitt, you are arrested for the killing of Jennifer Harrow. You unlawfully killed her, you do not have to say anything, but it may harm your defence if you do not mention when questioned something which you later rely on in court. Anything you do say may be given in evidence."

Just being read his rights made him panic; he felt like screaming *I've had enough just leave me alone*!

"You can go under the bail conditions." Adrian went out of the door. Adrian was in shock; he couldn't get out of the station quickly enough. He felt despair as if everything was bearing down on him. He walked towards home; everything was a blur. He went to cross a road and was nearly knocked down by a car and the driver used his horn; this mercifully woke him up and out of his shock at being charged. Right, he had got put, and he had some time to act but he needed to get on.

Jean called the sergeant over and said that she wanted him watched over the weekend. "He looks a bit panicked, let's see what he's up to."

Jean had had enough and went home.

\*\*\*\*\*\*\*\*\*\*\*\*\*\*\*\*\*\*\*\*\*

Jimmy Connor and his best friend David Caraway were riding their bikes around the track they used on the common.

It wound around in a circuit going through the trees and up and down ditches; the surface was compacted earth from the many cycles that used it. It was quite busy usually, and especially in the summer holidays, there were often 30 riders awaiting their turn. The circuit was in the woods that bordered the golf course. There was a footbridge over the railway line which ran beside the golf course. This railway line connected Croydon to Wimbledon and trams used it now instead of trains; there was another line which went from Streatham to Carshalton and was the main line to London.

The dress code was anything you wanted to wear-shorts and t-shirts were the norm. No one had a helmet of any sort. Accidents were usually the Elastoplast type but there had been a few broken bones. The boys had been speeding around the track not timing themselves, but pushing it, and enjoying themselves.

They stopped for a rest and nipped around to an ice cream van that was parked in the car park of the golf course. They bought some lollies from the ice cream man and went back to the starting point. They sat down on the grass to eat them. They laughed and joked with each other when looking into the wood Jimmy saw what looked like clothes, but something glittered and caught his attention. The boys went over and saw that next to the clothing was a mobile phone. Jimmy picked it up and it lit up but asked for a password to use. He put it in his pocket saying to David, "I'll give it to mum when we get home."

They carried on cycling the circuit, then they decided that they ought to go home, especially as they were both hungry.

On getting home, Jimmy gave the phone to his mother. She looked at it and saw it was an iPhone, so it might be worth a few bobs, so she would hand it in to the police the next day, and maybe Jimmy might get a reward for his honesty from the person who lost it.

The next day she took it into the police station saying that her son had found it on the common. She had to leave her details with them, The Desk Sergeant who new about the search being carried out on the common, rang Croydon Police and was put through to the murder team, He gave them the details of Jimmy's mother, including her address. He knew that she did not finish work till after 5:00 pm so home at about 5:30 give or take.

Jean was told that the phone had been found.

She arranged a car and she and Sergeant Walters left to talk to the two boys. They left early so they could collect the phone on the way. They pulled up outside her house which was a terraced property opposite a block of flats. There were toys and things in the garden along with a couple of well-used bikes. Jean knocked on the door and it was answered by a lady of about forty in a work-type smock; she had rubber gloves on which showed traces of foam from washing up. "Hello," she said questioning, "can I help you?" Jean showed her warrant card and was invited in.

"What's he done now?" She asked.

Jean smiled at her. "He's done nothing wrong that I'm aware of. You handed in a mobile phone that he found."

"Well, yes, he found it on the common."

"Well, we would like to talk to him about it, it is the mobile phone belonging to a young lady who was found dead on the common, one of the items she was without was her phone."

"Not the young girl who was murdered on the common."

"Yes."

"My boy has nothing to do with that, he's only eleven."

"Of course not, we just want to know exactly where he found it that's all."

She called the two boys in. They had been watching television in the other room. They came in and Jean smiled at them and asked them to sit down.

"Whereabouts did you find the phone?" She asked.

"By our adventure track."

"Where's that exactly?"

"Near the golf course, we could show you if you like."

"That's good of you, yes please."

Jean turned to his mother, "Is that ok? We won't arrest them but we may be a while."

"Yes, go ahead."

They all went in the police car. Jimmy told them it was near the golf course, so they drove to the golf course car park and parked there. "It's a Council Golf Course not a private one," Sergeant Walters said.

"Played there, have you?" Jean asked.

"Once or twice," said Walters.

They followed the two boys around to the adventurer circuit and David showed them where they had found the phone, the clothing was still there, "Did you find anything else like a necklace or ring?" Jean asked.

"No, we just found the phone."

The sergeant called in on his radio and asked for SOCO to attend the scene; they would stay there until they arrived.

The boys enthusiastically showed her the circuit pointing out the details. "Over that hump, you can get airborne."

"Golly," she said, "you are brave," wincing inwardly imagining these two young boys flying in the air on their bikes through the woods on this track.

She enjoyed chatting to the boys and they were enjoying chatting to her.

After about an hour, SOCO arrived and she left it to them to carry on with the scene and they walked back to their car.

"What's over that footbridge?" Jean asked.

"That's the bridge to the bomb site." David Said.

"Bomb site, what's that?" She asked.

"There is a load of half-bombed huts there."

The sergeant explained that there were a few bomb shelters there.

"Right, I want them searched too."

They drove the two boys back home and thanked them, and Jimmy's mother for their time and returned to the station.

The next day Jean went to the local bike store and bought two junior cycle crash helmets, she wrote a note thanking the boys again, and saying how impressed she was with their cycle track, but said that she would like them to wear these helmets, as she didn't want to hear that they were in hospital with injuries to their heads. She addressed them to their mothers and sent them off via parcel post along with a note saying how proud their mother should be as they were a credit to her and David's mother as well.

# Chapter 12

Later that morning, the phone was given to forensics for testing and to see what was on it. The people at the forensics found no fingerprints but the phone wouldn't open to reveal its contents as it had face recognition. This was difficult as one of the forensic team had to attend the morgue and hold the device to Jennifer's face, at which it opened, so the forensic guy changed the phone's way of opening in its settings so that it opened as soon as it was started. This way they could take their time with it.

The phone was interrogated, and all messages and pictures were downloaded and printed. The results were given to Inspector Jean.

*********************

Adrian went to the supermarket, he realised quickly that he was being followed. He had been looking out for it as soon as he had come out of his torpor. He was on the offensive now. He decided that he needed to get out and away. He sat at a table and made a list. Whilst he was doing that, he not only drank his coffee, but he also emptied the container on his table of all the sachets of tomato sauce, sugar, mayonnaise brown sauce and mustard and put them in his pocket. After finishing his coffee, he went shopping. He bought some tins of tuna in spring water, Spam, corned beef Cheddar cheese, a small bottle of olive oil, a small jar of mayonnaise, tea bags, dried milk, a pint of milk and went to the till and paid by card. On leaving, he went to the cash point and withdrew £250. He quickly put that into his pocket and walked rapidly to the house where he lived and to his room.

He made a cup of tea, sat down, and paused for a moment, got up and took a few biscuits, sat back down and relaxed for a bit, then he started getting things together, taking out his one-man tent. It went on the bed with a sleeping bag and fold-up water bottle which would take a gallon of water when full. He added to that his billy cans, and inside them was salt and pepper plus the sachets he had pilfered from the coffee shop. He also put in a polythene tube, which would help him fill the water bottle then added a trowel which was stainless steel with a retractable handle; also his knife, fork and spoon combo, and a sheath knife for all uses. Then his raincoat which he rolled up very small; then his clothing as much as he could carry and packed it in his kit bag. He put his compass, torch and matches in the pockets; then some fishing kit consisting of line weight hooks and float. He wasn't going to sit on the riverbank and fish nicely throwing the fish back in; he was going to poach. Using the pockets of his rucksack meant that he would be able to reach those items easily and quickly. Adrian then packed his small walking radio with earphones in another pocket. He rolled his clothing as much as he could as it took up less room than he had found.

His kit bag was put down beside the bed, then clipping his binoculars to it as he didn't have too much room, and took out his maps. He spent a long time pouring over them planning his route as much as he could, but he had to be flexible and ready to change his route as he needed.

He took out some writing paper and envelopes and thought about what he would write. He had decided that the future did not look good for him, so escaping for a while was all that he could do.

If things did not improve, in that the police did not arrest anyone else, then he would need to plan further. He thought that by hook or by crook that he would get to France which would then give him access to the continent. He would have to start learning another language, French or Italian maybe, he left his destination open but somewhere warm and sunny with warm seas, Italy, maybe. He could choose to go wherever he wanted and find somewhere to live in peace and quiet where no one knew him. He would have to live on cash and not have any bank cards as they were traceable, and he couldn't get another bank account in another name without an address.

He went to bed quite early and set his alarm to a silly time of 3:45 am in the morning to get up and be gone. He hoped he could get away unseen at that time; he wanted to avoid the shift workers who started at 6:00 am. Once gone, he was confident, they wouldn't get him easily. His knowledge of using native plants for food would keep him away from shops.

Adrian started to write the letter.

Dear Superintendent Roper

As I feel that I am the only suspect in this crime, I feel that I must try to keep out of jail, the best way I can. Please be assured that I am not guilty of this but feel that all the facts are against me.

I would plead with you to keep all options open and keep looking for the murderer, I repeat that it wasn't me.

Yours faithfully
Adrian Hewett

He addressed the letter to **Inspector Roper**
**Croydon Police Station**
**Croydon**
**Surrey**
He wrote a second letter to his place of work.
A & C Harris
Commonside East
Mitcham
Surrey
FAO John Sherwood

Hi John,

Expect you will have heard by now that for some reason the police have arrested me for murder. I can assure you that I am innocent but understand that you will have to sack me. Could I ask that my tools are all put away for me to pick up as soon as this is resolved?

Cheers
Adrian

# Chapter 13

He turned off his mobile phone, he had read that by leaving it on, his whereabouts could be traced. He turned the light off just in case someone was watching his window. He lay down on his bed and thought through what he was about to do, and what he was taking. He added pens and paper to his pack. He waited till 4:30 am, then got dressed except for his walking boots. He hoped that would be a good time to get out unseen. He went quietly downstairs in his socks to the backdoor, went out and put his boots on. He collected some boxes; there were always some around used by other residents of the house. He went back up and quietly put all his possessions in the boxes, taped them up and put his name on them PROPERTY OF ADRIAN HEWITT. That done, he went back downstairs replaced his boots locked up and was out.

He stood listening for a while to make sure all was quiet.

He crept down to the bottom of the garden and climbed over the wall which was six feet high, a small drop and he was in the allotments behind the house; he paused for a while listening and watching. All was still quiet, so he walked quickly over to one allotment and picked an apple off a tree. He walked through to the gate which was locked and quickly climbed over that and was in some playing fields. He followed the path around and sat down by a scout hut. On a wall, he was on a cinder track and off the road. He waited till 7:30, then he decided to change plans because he didn't want to give the police any idea where he was going, so he changed tack and walked through a park to Headcorn Road and onto the main road and walked down to Norbury Junction Railway Station; from there he bought a return ticket to West Croydon where he got off and walked to a nearby letterbox and posted his letter, then walked back to the train station and bought his ticket to Dorking West. He bought a return ticket again as there was only a few pence difference from a single ticket and would possibly keep them off his track for a bit longer. Going by train meant that he could buy tickets with cash, whereas he would have needed to use his card on a bus, and he didn't want to use them and give an indicator of where he might be going. With cash, he had left no paper trail for the police to follow. He walked along a corridor until he found the correct platform for Dorking, and then down some stairs to the platform; it wasn't very busy, as most people were heading the other way to London for work.

The train arrived, he got on it, put his kit bag on the rack above the seats and sat down, he was going to be in Dorking within the hour.

The train left smoothly and after the bustling Croydon, it moved into the beautiful scenery of farms and villages. He sat enjoying the cows, sheep and the occasional deer. It was the first time he had relaxed for a few days; it was as if he had a load taken off his mind. He knew it was only temporary, but he would make the most of it. By the time he neared his destination, he was up with kit bag on his back and ready to go. Adrenalin was pumping and he was ready to go.

As soon as the train stopped at Dorking West, he was off and away. He knew where he was going as he had walked this route not long ago and had decided to do the same thing, so he walked to the end of the road beside the station and walked into the fields. He took out his compass and map and his hip flask water bottle He knew the country code and would walk around the edges of fields. It made his journey a lot longer, but it would not annoy any farmer working his field as he didn't want any altercations. It was important that he kept under the radar. He headed first for Friday Street; this was a beautiful place with a large lake and pub, but turned away before reaching it, as it was also a well-known tourist spot, and set himself a course for Leith Hill and then from Leith Hill, walking across the country, avoiding people as much as he could. This meant keeping off the woodland paths if he could. He knew that there would be plenty of walkers whether it was a weekend or not, people took holidays to walk these routes or just to walk their dog.

At first, he was walking fast but after a few miles, he found himself walking at his old pace and although he knew he was a fugitive, he felt free, exhilarated, excited; wow he thought he hadn't expected that. The scenery was spectacular as ever undulating between fields, woods, and farms which gave him foresight on what or who was ahead; several times, he swapped the fields that he was going to walk through as he saw people walking in the distance.

As it was, he enjoyed walking across the fields; he put one earphone in his ear and turned on his radio for the news.

He started off walking quite quickly again. At 1:00 pm approximately, he sat down by a tree and ate the lunch which he had made earlier, cheese with tuna in mayonnaise sandwiches and some water from his hip bottle, delicious!

It was a pleasant day for a stroll; his aim was to get past Leith Hill and camp; he had looked on the map and found what he was looking for. A small central copse in the middle of a field there were many of these in the scenery of England, and the one he had found also had the bonus of a watering station for livestock; people thought that these water troughs were for animal use only and just contained rancid water, but Adrian knew these were filled from a ball valve situated under a cover which was part of the trough and was connected to the water main, so he would have fresh water for cleaning and drinking. He got up and started walking again. He took a long breath, he felt a form of excitement and relief, the walking in clean air and beautiful countryside lifted his spirits considerably.

At about 4:00 pm, he arrived near a village, Holmbury St Mary and decided to camp nearby for the night. He came across an allotment; there was someone working there so he found a place to observe him, and not be seen, he waited until he had finished, put his tools away and passed through the gates, got into his car and drove off. Checking that it was not overlooked and was empty of people, he delved into his pack and retrieved a bag and his trowel, then hiding his pack, he went in and quickly pulled up a few vegetables—a couple of large leeks, some potatoes, an aubergine. There was an apple tree which had eating apples, so he picked a few of them that were ripe. He quickly put them in his bag and went out the same way he came in. He had only taken one item from each holding so that hopefully the absence wouldn't be noticed except for the potatoes of course as he had to dig up one plant but got six potatoes of generous size.

He retrieved his kit bag and walked on for a couple of miles to where the copse he had identified was in view. He squatted down and watched for a while to make certain there was no activity, then walked across the field to an island of trees. He went into the copse getting a bit clawed by brambles and other thorny bushes. About 40 yards in, he found a clearing with enough room to put his tent up which didn't take him long. He put his sleeping bag down in it, then taking out his trowel, he scraped the ground to make certain there was no grass that could catch light from his small fire. He then placed stones around where the fire would be and then fetched some logs and brush and built his fire. He had a walk around the copse to see what was about, looking out from inside to see what was happening around, then went back and removed the water bottle that he had brought with him from his pack; it was the foldable one. He walked to the edge of the copse and checked there was nobody about and within sight of the water trough. Establishing that there was no one about, he quickly walked to the trough and filled his water bottle from the ball valve. He had brought a piece of polythene tube to help in this. He used the polythene pipe to bridge between the ball valve and his bottle, then quickly walked back to his tent.

He lit his fire from the matches he had brought with him, then removed the billycans from his pack. Inside the pans, he had placed salt pepper and a few other herbs, He had noted that there was fresh wild garlic growing, which was a plus.

The fire was ready now, so he put a billycan balanced on some old part bricks on the fire. He poured in water added salt and then the vegetables-potatoes first, then after waiting till they were practically cooked added the other vegetables and then cooked them till nearly ready, added the garlic which cooked quickly. He had only used enough vegetables for a meal, he opened the tin of Spam; he drained off the billy and still using the billy took out his knife, fork and spoon, which all came as a clip-together set. He hadn't wanted to use his tinned meat as he would need them later, but he needed it now. He ate the meal, he didn't particularly find it very tasty, but it filled a hole and he felt better afterwards. He finished off by making some tea, and after munching an apple which was sweet and tasty, the meal was finished nicely.

He washed everything up using his water container and swished it around and with his fingers cleaned his teeth, then put everything back in his kit bag ready to go at a moment's notice, if he had to he would leave the tent and sleeping bag but hoped he wouldn't have to. He didn't have to put out the fire as it had smouldered down to nothing. Then as it was getting dark, he climbed into his sleeping bag, zipped up the tent and was ready to go to sleep, He listened first to the radio until the news had ended, there was no mention of him now on the run, so he turned it off and feeling a little contented as he was in the open where he felt at home and with a full stomach, he fell asleep.

# Chapter 14

He woke the next morning, it was early, and the sun had not yet emerged. He had awakened slightly during the night hearing the foxes and other animals but not awakened completely. He got out of bed, watered the trees then dressed and scouted around to see what if anything was happening around him. His plan for the day hopefully was to hide his kit bag then he could walk unincumbered to sort out his main priority food for the day. He knew that there was a small river not far away, and with a bit of luck, he could fish there. As it was a chalk stream, he was hoping to get a trout which would be nice.

The last few days had taken a lot out of him, so he needed a rest day. He checked his map. His next camping point was at Ewhurst Green but hopefully Alfold, the River Tillingbourne ran around Alfold and across to the Mole Valley. He wanted to keep to this journey but was in no hurry unless pressed. He was in no rush now. He went back to camp, sat in his tent and turned on the radio, although there was mention of the murder, his name was not mentioned, they just said that a man had been arrested. He sat watching the bird life and listening to them twittering in the treetops, he had brought his binoculars with him so he could watch them; after all, he had nothing else to do. At, about 8:00 am, he checked once again for activity and there being none, he packed his gear away, taking down his tent and rolling up his sleeping bag. Then he hid his equipment up in a tree and went on his way. All he took was a fishing line hook, float and lure in a bag and off he went. It took him a couple of hours to get to a village store where he decided to chance his luck and bought butter; the girl on the tills was distracted by a local boy chatting to her which was good and he walked across the fields to where on the river he wanted to hide from the fish as well as people. It was where a small stone bridge crossed it; it was in a place where only the farmer and his livestock would use it going from one field to another as they were on opposite sides of the river, it wasn't on a public path which gave him some peace of mind.

*********************************

Jean looked at the transcripts from the phone and it was noticeable that Jennifer had enjoyed her hikes in the countryside; there were pictures of scenery, the group of walkers. It was the same people that had been interviewed already. There was nothing to bring anyone else to the forefront of the investigation.

"Have we heard anything else from forensics yet?" She asked.

"Yes, the reports just come in, and our people looked around the bomb site and found nothing. The clothes which consisted of leggings and knickers were a bit different, they have found carpet fibres on them and some other threads on the leggings."

"At least that's something," she said, "we will be able to check whether the location when we find it is the correct one. That is of course if we find a location."

"Were there any other details?"

"Yes, the fibres are from a new carpet red in colour or red with other colours, but they think mainly red as there were no other threads of other colours."

"Right, let's see if we can find a red carpet that's been delivered and or laid in this area in the last two months. Hopefully, there can't be too many."

"Can they say what sort of red, I mean there are many shades of colour red like maroon, or crimson?"

They are checking that now.

"Ok, well, let's still find if a red carpet of any sort of shade was bought, and where, and delivered to who?"

# Chapter 15

Adrian checked there was no one about. There wasn't, so keeping a low profile so as not to alarm the fish, he took out his fishing gear, he wasn't going to use his float, just his lure on a hook, the rest was a stick through the nylon thread and the lure was a trio of shiny chrome caps in line. He dropped it gently through the water. He was pleased to see watercress growing wild, from a local grower no doubt. After a few casts, he was rewarded with a trout attacking his lure. He gave the string a tug to engage the hook, then quickly pulled the flapping fish over the buttress, dispatched it quickly and put it in his bag; then quickly gathering some watercress, he went back to his copse. He got most of the way back when he came across a farmer working with a tractor in his field, so he had to circumnavigate it but it wasn't too much of a problem. On circling round to the opposite side to where he had seen the farmer, he ran across to the copse and crawled into where his tent was. He took out his billycans and filleted the fish and took off the head fins and tail, then put it in water with the butter and cress, put the lid on and put another bowl on top with water in so as to make an ad hoc refrigerator.

He sat down and immersed himself in the countryside, the birds singing and the sun breaking through the trees, whilst keeping an eye on the farmer on his tractor. He had to wait until the farmer had finished ploughing the whole field before he drove out of the gate, and left him in peace.

Some while later, he turned on his radio and listened to the news. There was still no mention of him, so he sat back quietly; he constantly hoped that he would hear of someone else being charged. All this would change he thought in the morning, they should get his letter, and realise that he was no longer at the house. If they had not already found out.

He made up his fire and put some potatoes on to boil having cut them into slices with leeks; once they were half-cooked, he used another billycan on the fire, put the fish in with the butter and cooked the potatoes to make into round chips. He also added the leeks which were half-cooked. After a while, he took it all off the fire and added more butter to them as well as the washed watercress. He thoroughly enjoyed his fish dinner and afterwards, he cleaned the billycans and put everything away.

He put up his tent and laid out his sleeping bag, light was falling, and darkness was approaching rapidly. He realised that he had been very fortunate with the weather, but it did not look as if the fine weather was going to continue. He had another apple, lay on his sleeping bag and relaxed. After finishing his apple, he walked around the copse and checked that all was ok, and there was no one about. He went back to his tent, zipped up the front, got into his sleeping bag and after listening to a play on the radio, he went to sleep.

During the night, the winds got up and rain lashed at the trees. He was fairly sheltered but it still woke him up. He wasn't sure whether he would move on in the morning; he didn't want to, in this weather, but he would wait and see.

When he woke up in the morning, it was to a different scene altogether. He opened his tent; the rain was dripping from the trees, and the wind blowing strongly. He added some more water to the trees and went back to his tent and snuggled back down again. He turned on his radio and listened to the news. No news again, so he got up, dressed, and put everything away, tent, sleeping bag everything. He had decided to move on the next day, so he was going to relax all day and save his energy. It was imperative though to be ready at the slightest sign that he was in danger of being discovered, that he was ready to move. He found a particularly dense tree growing where the rain did not reach the trunk and settled down beneath it.

He walked around the perimeter of the copse to check if there was anybody about, but he didn't expect so, not in this weather and he was right; there was no one in the fields anywhere.

That afternoon the rain abated for a while, so he decided to do a bit of foraging. He had no vegetables left to cook. He found some mushrooms, Hedgehog mushrooms; then he harvested some nettle leaves, the newer ones, adding wild crow garlic helped the taste, ensuring the soup would be nice and tasty, and he could make some soup.

Later, he started his fire with a little more difficulties due to the wet weather but once he got it going, it was fine. He washed the nettle leaves and crow garlic and added the mushrooms, then he put them in a bowl of water and boiled them, letting them simmer, he mushed them up as much as possible, then added salt and plenty of pepper. The result was a nice bowl of nettle soup which with the mushrooms and garlic went down a treat it was one of his favourites.

He still had some fruit to finish and had some beech tea which consisted of young beech tree leaves boiled in water and simmered for a while, he enjoyed that as well.

# Chapter 16

Inspector Jean arrived for work early.

"Any change, has anything happened?"

"No," she was told.

She went to her desk and as was her norm, opened her post. She came across the letter from Adrian; she opened it and read it, swore and called in Sergeant Walters.

She showed him the letter.

"I suppose that we still have people watching his place, and he hasn't been seen out and about?"

"I guess that's the case, should we send them in to see if he's there?"

"Yes, might as well but I'm not expecting to find him."

He radioed the police in the car outside, they went in and found him gone. They radioed back to give the news.

"Right," said Jean, "let's flush him out we know that he likes being outdoors and has been around the Dorking Leatherhead area, so let's put out a statement saying that we want him with a picture, and description and what he's wanted for. Also, that he may well be in the Dorking area."

"Right, will do."

"Let's get whatever we can about him. Has anyone been to his work? He's worked there some time, so he must have made friends there or the people that he worked with must have impressions of him. Let's get three DCs down there to find out. Out of courtesy, we will contact the manager to let him know we are coming."

She sent the three detectives to the works at Commonside East, Mitcham. The surroundings were noisy, at one end, there was a machine shop with a fair amount of noise coming from there. At every corner were welding bays where the welders were noisily hitting the metal with chipping hammers taking the slag off of welds. Then there was a sheet metal area where sheets of steel from 16swg to 6mm thick stainless steel, steel, and aluminium, all being cut on guillotines and shaped on various other machines. Then there was the fitting shop where the pieces were put together and finished ready for shipment. They only made custom machinery here, made to measure. Apparently, Adrian had worked in every department and was now working as a fitter, sometimes going out to install the machines. The detectives were allowed by the management to wander around safely with a foreman as a guide to ask their questions about the workforce.

There were no bad words about him, most enjoyed his company, and he would attend the pub at dinner hours with a group that went there daily. They did find out that he went to college one day per week; so that was something else they could look at. They came away with nothing of use to them.

"Blimey, no wonder he likes to spend time in the country, it's so noisy here," said one DC.

They phoned the college and asked about him, but he had finished there last year, so there were no people there now who knew him, other than a couple of training staff.

So, they returned to the station with nothing new.

Adrian thought about what he would do if they, the police, didn't find the person who had committed the murder.

He put up his tent and got his sleeping bag unrolled and settled down for the night with still nothing on the news again, he fell asleep.

The morning dawned overcast and rainy again; he packed everything in his kit bag, shaking his tent to remove some drips but overall, his tent was dry. He covered his kit bag with a plastic weather protector that he kept for bad weather. All packed, he walked the perimeter again to check for any sign of life, but again there was no one about, so he put his kit bag on his back. The only thing he kept out were the apples; they were tasty and would last well. He went across the field to its edge; it was pretty muddy but better than he had thought he hoped that the rest of his journey would be okay. The ground was pretty solid; he knew that it was going to take some time to get the next part of his escape accomplished. He realised that passing through farm fields and walking around them would take a considerable time, where the grass was short and nothing had been planted. He would walk across them; he had his radio on and was listening to it with one earphone; the reason for one earphone was so that he could hear what was going on around him. He was using his compass now as he was uncertain of the route having not been here before.

He tramped on, being dripped on by the trees and the water from his hooded top dripping down and tickling his nose. The miles were going a lot slower today and then he heard it, and it stopped him dead in his tracks. The news had come on and they started talking about the murder and then interviewed Inspector

Roper. She said that they were looking for a suspect who was bailed and had left his home and could be practically anywhere in the UK but had connections to Dorking and Leatherhead. She appealed to him to give himself up to the police; she also said that enquiries were still progressing.

It took his breath away, he felt vulnerable, and it was a few minutes before he could concentrate on walking.

For most of that day, it was all he could do to put one foot in front of the other. He got to Ewhurst but did not venture into the village itself; he quickly crossed roads waiting until the coast was clear before haring across.

He got to a field with a copse in the centre. He walked to it and found a way into a small clearing. He quickly put up his tent rolled out his sleeping bag and lay down on top with the radio on. He forced himself to relax, he had only an apple to eat, so he tucked into it; the apple's taste seemed to perk him up. He made himself think positively and felt better for it. He had heard the weather forecast which followed the news was for a clear day tomorrow, he hoped that it would be dry at least. He was moving away from the Dorking, Leatherhead area, so hopefully away from the police's prime search area.

He was heading for Rowly or just above it on the map, he would cross the Wey South Path and there was a footbridge over the river and a couple of fields away was a triangular copse in the corner of a field as part barrier from the adjoining field. He took his compass readings and was ready for an early start the next morning.

6:00 am and he was up, watered the trees, cleaned his teeth; he had run out of water, so he just brushed and spat, he put his kit bag on his shoulders and started off. As said on the weather forecast, the clouds were scattered and the sun broke through. He started at a fair pace and was soon making good headway. Keeping to his compass heading and by lunchtime, he looked around for a sighting so that he could check his location. He sat down and ate his last apple, then was off and walking, afternoon came and about 4:00 pm, he reached the Wey South Path which had signposts. He knew he was on track and felt a lot better now, his spirits were lifted.

He crossed the river by the bridge, he could see it was quite deep and clear. Once he got to the copse, he slipped through the barbed wire which surrounded it and found a place for his tent which he put up and laid his sleeping bag out. He took out his shopping bag which had the fishing gear in and another bag containing his dirty clothes. Adrian went back to the river, still no one about, so he took out his dirty clothes and washed them in the water just rinsing them through as he did not have any soap.

Then on looking around, he checked that he could see a good distance to get an early warning of anyone coming, He stripped off quickly and went quickly to the water's edge; he quickly waded in until it reached his waist then dived forward and swam a bit diving down to wash his hair. He didn't spend as long as he wished but it was very cold. He got out quickly, towelled himself off with a towel he had brought with him and dressed again. He felt refreshed.

Next in the order of things was food, whilst it was clear he took out his fishing gear, went beside the bridge and threw his lure out and then gently pulled it away. He had to do this a dozen times but with people walking towards him in the distance, he had a bite and as quickly as he could pulled the fish in. It was a rainbow trout, about a pound in weight; he quickly bagged it and grabbed his clothes and quickly disappeared into the fields and back to his copse. He placed the trout in a billycan after gutting it and cutting off the head and tail. He could see the cattle trough in the middle of the field, so when the people had passed by, he took his water vessel and filled it up, then went back and put some water on the fish and billy on top. He looked at his map to see where the nearest allotments were. They were far away, and it was beginning to cloud over and getting dark. He had get his fire ready for lighting and made his way across the fields to some scrubland. He sneaked in and after exploring a bit and making certain that all the people had gone, he dug up some dandelions root and all with his trowel, and pulled up some hedgehog mushrooms. He had some wild watercress from the river. There were no apple trees but plenty of plums growing wild on the trees which he put in his bag. He went back to camp, hung his washing out in the tree's branches and started his fire.

He cooked the potatoes, then the fish to which he added the dandelions and put them in the billy with the butter he had bought the other day. He baked until ready, then scoffed the lot, he hadn't realised how hungry he was.

He washed up afterwards and put everything away and climbed into his sleeping bag. He listened to the radio and thought that he was safe, for the present. He felt clean and was happy that he was on schedule. He knew he couldn't stay here long, as there were too many people about. He was still shocked at hearing the radio broadcast, naming him as the suspect and even saying where they thought he was. He realised that although he was on the right side of the Dorking area, it was imperative that he moved quickly away, and put in some miles tomorrow. On the other hand, he had to maintain keeping concealed from other walkers.

# Chapter 17

He slept well and woke refreshed and ready to go. He packed everything up in readiness. He cleaned his teeth and then went to the barbed wire. All of a sudden, he stopped. There was a tractor heading his way, He crouched down and watched as the farmer started ploughing his field; he could possibly have got out the back but it was in the wrong direction, it would also take him near more people which he definitely didn't want. It wasn't a big field, so the ploughing should be finished quite quickly, and it was.

It was later than he hoped to start but at least, he was off. He went quickly across the field; well, around it. He didn't want his boots caked in mud, that would make for uncomfortable walking. His next objective was Frillinghurst Wood passing north of Chiddingfold. He realised that he would be hard-pressed to get to where he wanted to finish, so he would need to set a fast pace. At first, that was ok and he became optimistic, then he came to a few fields where men were working in them. He had to go around them keeping low and hoping no one saw him.

He had forgotten for a while to check behind him, and when he did, he was shocked to see that someone was following him. The pack that he had on his back prevented him from running away, so he thought quickly. There were some woods up ahead, so he would try to get there as fast as he was able to, without appearing from behind to be increasing his pace, so he maintained his pace, but increased the length of his stride and hoped to get to the wooded area as fast as possible. The trouble was he did not know what was in store for him in the woods.

He reached them at last, he hadn't had time to look at his map so was unsure of what faced him ahead. Adrian entered the woods with about a quarter mile between him and the follower. It was obvious now that the person who was after him was following but not intending to catch him, it was still a problem as he had to lose him well before he got a fix on the direction he was heading in, and so where he was camping. There was a main path through the woods which was well-worn and with rubble on its surface. A couple of hundred yards in was some crossroads; he did a left and hurried down about a hundred yards and went carefully off to the right, to do a left would bring him back into the opposite direction to his original direction. And meant that he would need to watch in case he came across the follower ahead of him. He was in the trees now and in quite a dense woodland, which was of pine trees, they had been planted in rows so it was a man-made wood. He travelled a small distance, there was little light here and the trees were close together and spread thickly which was good for his flight.

He stopped behind some, which gave him ample cover but enabled him to see back to the main path he had recently left. He saw the follower pass by, so waited a minute or two, then continued the way he had been going. He made his move, continuing through the trees, which was a little noisy but he carried on walking in the same direction until he reached a clearing. It was a long slender space and in its place, there was a stream about eight feet across but moving quite slowly. He sat down in cover and took off his boots and socks and waded across the stream as quickly as he could. Either side of the stream was a bit marshy, so taking his boots off had been a must; on reaching the other side, he sat again in cover and dried his feet off and cleaned off the mud as much as possible on some moss, he then went into the woods again and sat for a while, to let the follower give up, he hoped!

After a while, he carried on walking and a short distance later came to a lane. There was traffic, but he waited patiently until it was clear, then hurried across and into a wood on the other side. Adrian stopped again and checked his map, fortunately, he was still going in the right direction and further came across a footpath which was going in the right direction.

He came to a stile and quickly clambered over it. The further he walked, the more people he saw and had to avoid. After walking for some time and hoping that people would become scarcer, he decided that he would have to make the best of it and find somewhere to pitch his tent and lay low for a while. He was climbing Hascombe Hill now, he walked around the hill fort there and looked in the trees for a place to stay for a while. He decided to go a fair way into the wooded area to avoid dog walkers. The ground wasn't particularly flat, but he found a place where he could sit and remained there for a while. He looked in the bag containing the plums he had picked, a couple had ripened, so he ate them; they were sweet and juicy. He watched the birds flying around, he recognised a couple of Buzzards. They perched up in one of the taller trees; he loved watching birds of prey and these were certainly no exception. They were obviously a pair and were building a nest; watching them was peaceful and he enjoyed it. At first, he had just used his eyes but now he was using his binoculars for a clearer picture.

Suddenly, he thought that they had become vultures and were watching him; bloody hell, his imagination was playing tricks on him.

It didn't seem to quieten down until 8:30 pm and he decided that he would have to get out of this area as quickly as possible. He had been constantly listening to his radio to keep abreast of his situation as much as possible. He was lucky that there was a full moon, so he would have some light to help him get through what was left of the rest of this leg of his journey. He got up and started on his way. He decided that the best way to get near to his next objective was going to be using the roads as this would enable him to get a bit of speed up without falling flat on his face. At the same time, he had to keep out of sight of anyone and everyone; this had been a particularly busy place during the day and he needed to get back to more deserted scenery.

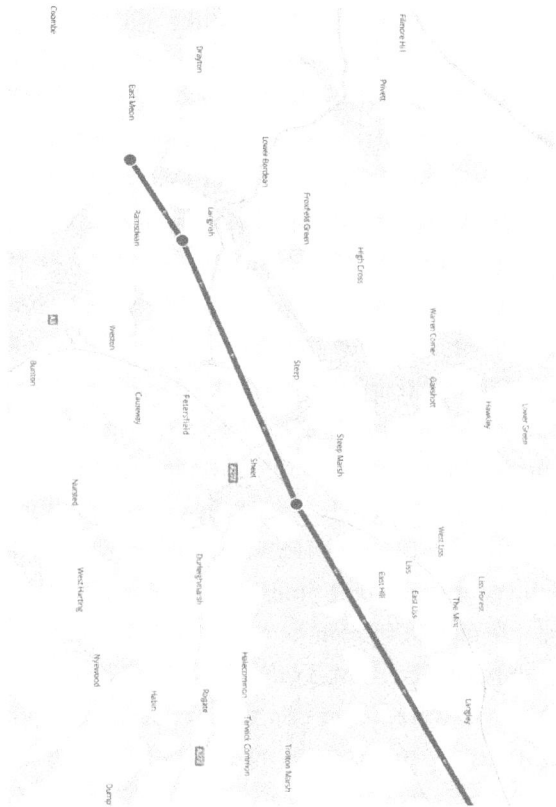

He took his small torch out of his pocket. He wasn't going to use it to light his way but needed to look at his map and compass every now and then. He got to Vann Copse without incident and continued. He skirted south of Northbridge and came eventually to the A283; there was traffic, but he waited for an empty space and hared across the road and into the brush on the other side. He walked through the Downs and looked at the allotments there. He stopped there to get some food for a couple of days, digging up some potatoes, leeks, onions, carrots and swede. He managed to scrump some apples, packed it all away and exited the allotments, checked his map again and carried on his way. He came at last to Pheatons Copse and looked about for somewhere to stay. He just rested until the sky lightened so that he could look around, then found a flat hidey hole, pitched his tent, rolled out his sleeping bag and lay down and slept. He was very tired, and it hadn't taken him long to fall asleep. It was 11:00 am according to his watch when he woke up hearing voices, he looked out of his tent and could see a couple of women and their dogs walking. It appeared that the dogs had taken off into the woods, probably on the scent of deer or rabbit; they were walking away from him, so he just watched them quietly.

When all was quiet, he stood up and went for a walk around to scout out the area. He walked the perimeter and then through the centre. Several times, he was forced to take cover whilst people passed by, but he remained unseen, he returned to his tent hungry and delved into his bag of plums and ate the ripe ones. There were only a couple left that weren't going off and afterwards, he threw them away. He hadn't thought that it would be this busy in one of the copses he had picked, and fervently hoped it was the first and last time he picked one that was this busy; this one even had a path through it.

# Chapter 18

Sally Parsons rang the station and was put through to Jean, "Hello," she said. "I told you that I would think about who she didn't like at all and who she had seen recently."

"Yes, you did, have you come up with someone?"

"Yes," she said, "I might have."

"It was that yesterday I saw someone I believed had +emigrated to Australia. He was a bit of an annoyance to Jennifer, they used to hate each other at school, and even at college; he tried it on with her a couple of times and wouldn't take no for an answer. She ended up using her knee to make him stop, that worked but it made him very angry. What do you think, I mean it's funny that he should pop up near us when we have moved fifty miles away."

"It sounds to me that there is no harm in looking at him, of course, we won't mention your name."

"His name was Ronnie Tyler, that's all I can tell you but I've seen him twice in Norbury High Street. That's all I can tell you."

"That's ok. Thank you for your call."

Jean called out to all the people in the office. "Right, people, we need to look at this man, find him, and where he lives, At the same time, we need to look at whether he is one of the people who bought a red carpet."

They looked through people who had bought a carpet with no luck; they looked on the election register and found nothing.

They checked everywhere they could think of and could find no sign of him. They looked at whether there was a record of him coming back into the country.

Nothing!

Right, either Sally was mistaken about his identity or there was something else happening.

They investigated Australian records to find when he got into the country and found that he had left the UK for Melbourne, Australia a few years earlier.

Jean rang up the Melbourne Police and spoke to a detective chief there, she explained why she was ringing and whether they had a record or anything about the man, she gave his full name. Ronnie Tyler; there was a pause and then the chief said that he would put her through to a detective inspector, but unfortunately, he wasn't in the building, but he would ring her when he got back.

From that, Jean had the impression that he was known to the police there, so was interested to know why.

Inspector Johnston of the AFP Australian Federal Police rang Jean thirty minutes later.

"Hi," he said, "I understand that you're interested in Ronnie Tyler."

"Yes," she said, "we are wondering if he is still in your country or come back to ours."

"We are wondering the same."

"I gather that he is a person of interest to you as well. Is that right?" Jean asked.

"Yes, we are looking at the death of the woman he was living with, she disappeared under suspicious circumstances and we want to talk to him about it. What's your beef with him, if I may ask."

"Well, we want to talk to him about murder too, but we have the body. But we don't have any evidence of him coming back to the UK."

"He has some very dodgy contacts and it's quite possible that he got hold of a forged passport."

"Ok, thanks for that, we will keep looking for him, we've only just started. Can you send me any files you have on him please?"

"No problem," he said.

"I'll keep in touch," she finished.

"Thanks," he said, "so will I."

# Chapter 19

He listened to the radio and heard that he was still wanted but he wanted to contact them desperately to let them know he was still in the country and to tell them again that he was not guilty. He knew he couldn't do that, or they would have him.

He gathered some wood and built his fire, not lighting it till later. He also needed water, so towards nightfall, he made his way to the edge of the trees, the trough was behind a barbed wire fence. When he was sure it was clear, he went across to it and filled his water container up and zipped back to the wire, then put his water underneath the fence. He managed to get back over and get back amongst the trees. On getting back to camp, he prepared his veg, and getting his billy out, placed potatoes and swede in it with a little salt and he was ready to start cooking. As the last vestiges of daylight disappeared, and darkness began to press, he lit his fire and set his billy on to boil. After they had boiled and were simmering, he put the second billy on with carrots and leek cut up in it. After they cooked, he put them into one billy, added half his tin of corned beef and ate from that. He had a little oil left, so sparingly added it to the meat; then using the second billy, he boiled some water to make his tea.

He was very hungry as he had not had much since the day before. He finished his meal sitting by the fireside eating an apple and drinking his tea. He washed up and put his billy's and eating utensils away and was ready for the next day. He was hoping to stay put for another day to rest his tired muscles and he was still a bit tired from the happenings of the day.

He went to his bed tired but with his stomach full, he listened to his radio and after the news, fell asleep. He had heard them warning the public that he was still about and that he had been quite often in the Dorking Betchworth Leatherhead triangle, so the police were looking especially there and abouts. It was the abouts that worried him; he had moved out of the specific area they had said he may be hiding in, but he was on the periphery and needed to move away. He decided that he would need to listen out for helicopters as well as people searching. Helicopters had good cameras on them as well as the type that could find heat sources. He hoped that they couldn't see the difference between a human and a deer. He managed to sleep through the night even though there were many sounds from wildlife.

Waking in the morning, he checked his watch and saw it was about 7:00 am, so quickly got up and ready to move should the need arrive.

Not far from Petersfield now, his next objective was to get around the town as where he was it was quite busy. Petersfield is a largish town and spread out so took some getting around. He decided to go at once, he packed up his tent and sleeping bag, shouldered his kit bag and set off. He was soon at the barbed wire fence and putting his kit bag through it, he climbed over the top. Shouldering his kit bag again, he set off across the field as it was a grass meadow; there was a gate at the end which led into another field. He later skirted Heath Farm and carried on around Petersfield, across a road, then skirted a golf course keeping well back as they were always busy. He walked for quite a while then stopped for a while at Bolling Hill Copse for a rest and to check his bearings on the compass. Setting off again, he found a tunnel under the A3 then moved Northwest to Widow Knights Copse, which was his next objective. As ever, he moved quickly around the copse to make certain it was safe. There were places around it that he could not reach due to dense vegetation, but he thought it was safe. He went back and erected his tent and sleeping bag, then trowelled the grass to make certain that his fire couldn't spread, then settled down with an apple.

As soon as it was dark, he lit his fire and had the same meal that he had eaten the day before he faced looking at his map. He knew that the next stage of his journey was going to be hazardous regarding people traffic. There was a large population in this area, and they all seemed to be out taking their pets for walkies.

Even where he intended to camp was quite risky, he was heading for the Itchin Valley.

Early morning and up he got ready to go. He walked out of the copse and into farmland, skirting the arable fields and hurrying across the pastures; he was pleased with his morning walk so far. He passed south of Ramsden and Oxenborne House and Farm and across Small Down; it wasn't too big a hill but still took his breath away. He had a little stop to eat another apple and get his breath back. Taking care, he passed coombe and castle cottages. At Stock Lane Farm, he changed course slightly. He crossed Frys Lane and went north past Meonstone House. Not too far now, just a few miles more. At last, he reached Galley Down; he didn't feel that it was very safe here, so he carried on to Durley Copse. He could see from the map that there was a river there. He walked around the edge to make certain it was safe, then returned and put up his tent and settled down for the night. The only food he had was an apple, which he ate hungrily and lay on his sleeping bag and listened to his radio. He didn't bother making a fire as he was only intending to stay the night and had nothing to cook. He was getting more and more despondent as there was no change in the investigation of the murder, and he went to sleep in that vein of thought.

The next morning he woke before dawn and got ready to move; this was going to be a testing day. He walked between Corhampton and Meonstoke as quickly as possible, then on to Galley Down where he had a little rest; then he kept just South of Ashton then skirting around Wintershill to Durley Copse, Walking past Horton Heath, he kept to the north, then quickly taking a risk, he took the tunnel under the railway and into Hog Wood.

Then he reached his next camping point at Milkmead Copse, which was close to Itchen Country Park. He would have to be careful here as he was near to where day-trippers could be. He erected his tent and settled down for the night; there was plenty of noise as he was next door to Southampton Airport and the planes continued to about 10:00 pm. He slept through till about 6:00 am, then got up and got going. His main objective was to get around the airport and into Lakeside Country Park through North Stonecamp, then Bracen Hall under the M3 M27 interchange into Hut Wood and across to Long Copse where he had enough walking and found a nice spot and put up his tent and got his fire ready. He waited till darkness was falling, then he took his bag and walked to where he could see allotments on his map. He dug up a few potatoes, onions, carrots and seeing an apple tree, he took some of them down and put them in his bag. Next, he went back to the River Test. This was a beautiful chalk river with wild watercress, so he picked some of that and then took out his fishing gear. It took him over an hour before he caught anything but then he caught a nice-sized brown trout. He quickly dispatched it, put it in his bag and then going back to his camp, he placed the food in his tent while he went to fetch water from another horse trough.

He decided to go back to the river for a quick dip, it was freezing cold, but boy, did it do him good. He towelled himself off quickly and went back to his tent; he was tingling all over. It was dark by the time he was ready to cook. He prepared his veg and fish, then put his potatoes on to boil; then cooked his fish with everything else. He had a little oil left, so put some with the fish and onions and carrots; washed the watercress put everything together and tucked it in. He was famished. After finishing every scrap, he washed up and put everything away, then sat down on his bedding and munched through his apple. He lay down and thought through his next steps; he wouldn't allow himself to think of anything else, he had to concentrate on what was to come. He fell asleep, feeling a bit better now; he had a full stomach.

# Chapter 20

He slept a little late the next morning. One thing that he had noticed was that his reflection had changed in the water of the Test. He saw that he had a good growth of a beard, he had got through the itching phase and felt ok now. He got all his gear together and started over the river. He took a footbridge over the Test and ran across a bridge over the motorway and across to Golden Gutterthrough Stonyford down to Winsor and further to Brockishill Enclosure. He was in the New Forest at last.

He didn't have any dinner that night and just lay down in his tent with a couple of apples; he couldn't quite understand it but he felt sad, for no particular reason. He started off again along the Millyford Bridge path, following the A35 but just keeping out of sight of it. He got to Wilverley Inclosure; not far to go now. He carried on walking. He saw other walkers in the distance, but none drew close. He walked on and through Broadlea enclosure; he really wanted to go through set thorns enclosure but found that there was a large campsite for caravans which meant a lot of people, so it was a place to be avoided. He walked close to Sway and went through farms. As he had come out of the forest proper, he went past the

Sway tower which he could see from a distance and it served well as a landmark for checking his compass directions.

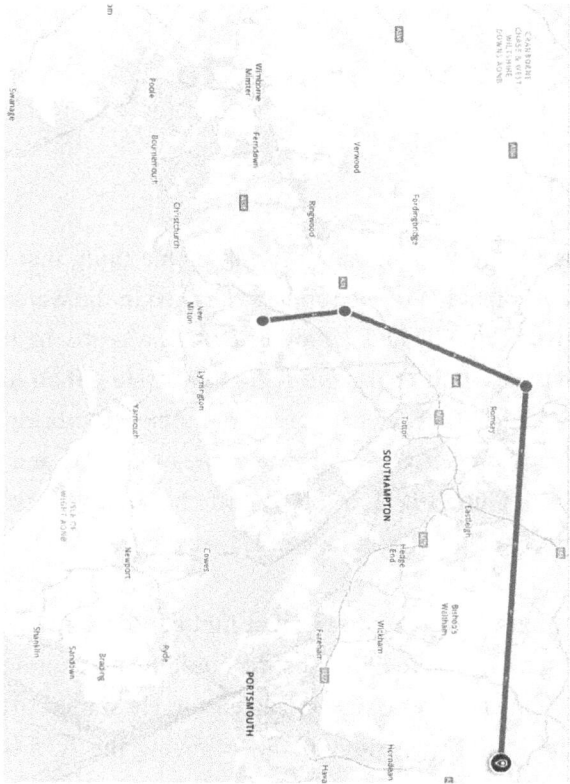

He reached his target, Barrows Copse at last and walked around it and carefully. It was a triangular copse sited at the end of a field which was in turn next to the road to Lymington. Adrian set out his tent and sleeping bag, then made out his fire, he didn't light it, but it was ready to go. He was more unhurried than at previous sites as he intended to stay here long term. He didn't bother with dinner that night but just relaxed his aching muscles. All in all, he was knackered.

He had, at last, reached his first objective, to reach the coast and be near the New Forest; it was now his intention of getting himself into the locality proper. He couldn't just keep on the run with no contact with other humans, he needed to talk and meet people.

This was going to be hard, it had been hard enough to run away, whether he was right or wrong to do that, but now would be the riskiest time as he was planning to integrate locally.

# Chapter 21

It had been an epic journey and going around the perimeters of fields had added many miles. He ate an apple and went to sleep. He listened to the news and found that they were still searching for him and there were no new developments.

He woke up in the morning and thought about his plans; he had no intentions of taking vegetables from local allotments as he intended to stay there for a while. He did not want to draw attention to himself. He would use his knowledge of things he could find growing and use them to make some reasonable meals. He made himself a list of what he needed from the shops He was about to walk into the open sporting a new beard which had grown well over the period whilst he was on the run, and a while before. He hoped that would be enough; he wouldn't be using his kit bag so he didn't look like a traveller but more of a local. He wrote a shopping list. He wanted olive oil, vinegar, mayonnaise, tins of tomatoes, beans, milk just a pint for now and some powdered, that was it. He took his shopping bag and walked to the supermarket at Lymington that was quite a walk if he was going to do that daily, but he had no intentions of doing that. He collected the items on his shopping list and used some of his cash which he had been careful with.

He found the notice board which had postcard sales on it; he found two things he was interested in-a bicycle and a fishing rod with gear. There were two different cards for bikes, and they were both at about £30 and the fishing gear was £40. He noted the phone numbers and walked down the road to where a phone box stood. He rang up and talked first of all to the bike owners. He wanted a largeish frame and was satisfied that one was what he wanted and arranged to go round then and there as it was very near. He also rang up for the fishing gear and was pleased that they were in and it was also close by, he arranged to go round as soon as he had been to see the bike.

His future plans were for a lot of fishing with the correct gear for catching sea fish; catching the freshwater fish was one thing but, in the ocean, fish could be more selective of baits and also he needed to be able to pull them in from the sea, so needed a proper rod for that, not just a stick, or the line would take his fingers off.

He arrived at the house selling the bike and checked the bike out, it was good and nice to ride; he managed to pay £25 and they were pleased that he paid cash. The fishing gear was next, he was pleased that it contained a good rod, reel, and all the rest of the relevant gear. He bought, it but the owner wouldn't take less; it was fair enough really, so he paid for it, secured the shopping bag around him, and tied the rod to his bike; all being accomplished, he cycled back to his camp site, he had to take care as the way home was on well used roads first of all and he didn't want to be stopped by police as he was riding it in a dangerous condition, walking the bike through the field nearby, lifting it over the barbed wire fence and settled it near his tent.

It was close to nightfall and he lit his fire, whilst in the supermarket he had bought a few things not on his list. A tin of curry and sachet of rice, some russet apples and most importantly, a large bottle of St Miguel lager. He put his billy on the fire and started his meal of beef curry and a sachet of rice; he cooked the rice first, then emptied the tin into another billy and cooked that and then sat back against a tree and ate his meal and drank his lager, luxury. He had forgotten about water and had to go and fill his water container up from an animal trough. He could then wash up and put everything away in case he had to move fast.

He went into his tent, got into his sleeping bag and put the radio on, then went to sleep. The next morning, he was up and stirring the fire back to life, he made himself a nice cup of tea using his milk; it was ecstasy. He heard on the radio that it was the day of the funeral. He was saddened that he couldn't be there but told himself that he would go to her grave when and if he ever got home. It saddened him that he had been unable to mourn her loss properly. She had been a good friend and he would miss her. He thought about who else could have been involved. They had some good times walking together and as a group, getting out of the built-up area and into the countryside they'd had some good laughs when something untoward happened; like him losing the way or something they would sit and laugh at. Even though it took some time to get back on track, they had shared their packed lunches, it had been a good break to the week and they had been going over a year now, not every week, but when they could.

It broke his heart that she had gone now just like that, and there was no closure for him, nor would there be.

Jean and a few of the other detectives went to the funeral in Basingstoke, out of courtesy and to show that they felt some of the pain that her mother was feeling. Jean had contacted all the walkers except of course Adrian, and they went as well.

It was a nice service and afterwards, they all went to a local pub where refreshments were laid on. Jennifer's mother was still very tearful, but made a bee line for Jean to find out how the case was progressing.

Jean told her that it was progressing well, and they hoped to have a suspect in custody very soon.

Jennifer's mother thanked them for coming.

She then went on to meet and talk to other people her daughter had enjoyed walking with. Jean and the detectives left as soon as they felt they were able to, going back to the police station in Croydon, they carried on their investigations.

**********************

He got his fishing gear out and sorted it out for what he wanted to take today; he took the bike across the field, strapped the rod back on the bike and cycled off.

He cycled down to the front and took the path down to the bottom and found a nice place by the rocks, Adrian started casting, he knew this might take all day he had a float on now and a lure on the line; he had no food for the fish, so it was this or nothing. It was nice to fish at last in the sea and not have to worry about anyone catching him.

He sat there for hours, he rested the rod on some rocks for a while and looked around for anything else that would go with the fish, he found some native samphire he didn't pick any, it was no good without a fish; at last, he had a bite and struck quickly. He reeled in the fish; it took a while but was a mackerel. He dispatched it quickly and put it in his bag, put his rod away and collected some wild samphire and some seaweed, then cycled back, had a quick look round to make certain that there was no one about, then pushed his bike back to his camp.

He started his fire as soon as darkness closed in and put some oil in, gutted his fish and removed the head tails and fins; instead of disposing of them, he put them in a plastic bag; they would be the bait for the morrow. He butterflied the mackerel, cutting it in half down its length, and opened it up and laid its skin up in the billy. He put in the samphire and some washed seaweed; then after a few minutes, he turned the fish over and cooked the other side, then took it off the fire and ate it avoiding the bones. He didn't eat the skin but enjoyed his dinner and made a cup of tea with an apple, his favourite variety, Russet. He put the radio on whilst he ate but there was nothing new.

He had to think about what he would do if he could go back home knowing he didn't face arrest, He had already heard via the news that his employers had cancelled his contract of employment, so he was jobless. He could now no longer pay his rent, so he would be homeless as well, but to look at the other side, if they found him guilty, he wouldn't have to worry about housing, he would be in jail. So what could he do? He realised that when they found that he was not guilty, he would face another kind of penalty homelessness and bankruptcy, so what could he do? He knew that his bank account held about £200; he needed to increase that for a start. He had heard that a person needed a domestic address to have a bank account, but as he already had a bank account that would be ok, as long as he didn't inform them of the change of address. He would advertise on the supermarket boards as an odd-job man and gardener, so that was one thing he could do. When he went home, he would look for a flat or room in a house and then look for a job. He couldn't go on the dole as he couldn't let them know where he was.

He needed to sort these problems out as soon as possible.

So the next morning, he would start by buying a pack of postcards, then he would go fishing as yesterday. He had liked the place where he fished, so would go there again. It was important now to bury himself in the community and hide in plain sight. Then he could sit and write his postcards out, and of course, he also needed a mobile phone, an unregistered one where he paid for the minutes he used, with no trail to him. To this end, he went to the local supermarkets and bought a small phone; all he wanted was a phone and text nothing else, so it was cheap. He bought a card which put £10 on the phone, that would last him a while he hoped. His funds were going down quite quickly now.

Adrian went to a corner shop which was close to him and bought a pack of postcards.

# Chapter 22

He returned to where he had fished before and using the bait that he had put in a polythene bag, he sat back for a long wait. He wasn't disappointed and caught nothing for about two hours, but he was in no rush. Then he had a bite; he struck quickly and was surprised how strong this fish was. He reeled it in eventually and found it was a large Bass; he was overjoyed, this would be a good feast for tonight. He again took some wild samphire and seaweed and put them all in his bag. There was no one about and the beach wasn't overlooked, so he undressed and swam for a while. Refreshed from his swim, he dried himself off and got on his way back to his camp. There was no one about so he dismounted quickly and wheeled his bike quickly over the field, over the barbed wire and sat down next to his tent; he took a chance and relit his fire and boiled some water and made some tea. Then he composed what he wanted to put on the postcards. He spent the rest of the day keeping watch around his site, all seemed peaceful.

That evening, he was pleased with his fish dinner; he listened to his radio, no mention of the murder again but the weather report which came on after the news, told him to expect really bad weather coming in through the night. That night he went to sleep but at about 2:00 am, he was woken up by thunder, lightning and torrential rain; he snuggled down in his sleeping bag and listened to the rain hammering down on his tent and occasional thunder.

The ground in the morning was very wet and the rain was continuing. He wasn't going anywhere that day.

It poured down all day so he did nothing but lay on his sleeping bag and thought about Jennifer. He would miss her; like the time they had come to the side of Box Hill that you didn't want to walk down; it consisted of trees and foliage going very steeply down the chalky slope at the bottom of which was the River Mole. Jennifer had slipped at the bottom and had landed in the river. She didn't go far in and just got a little wet; her boots in particular. Another time, they came across a circular tarmac area and it wasn't till she stepped on it and sank up to her ankles that they realised that it was sewage, they had somehow walked onto the edge of sewage works. She stank and they had laughed a lot about it and they had made her walk someway behind them; fortunately, they came past a gentleman watering veg in his garden and he laughingly hosed off her feet and shoes, which fortunately were plastic. That was just one of the times they had laughed with her.

They had really enjoyed their walks; all of them. The group would probably have got bigger with more people joining them but that wouldn't happen now.

The rain stopped but Andrew didn't think that it would be long before it started again; he hoped that it would be better on Sunday as it was the day of the car boot sale and he needed to get some equipment for gardening.

He had seen posters advertising it on the notice board by the supermarket, it wasn't far away, and he would be travelling by bike.

He quickly took his bike over the field and down the road to get to the supermarket. He first took his postcards to the desk and paid for them to be put up for a month. Then looked quickly at the offers; he saw a plastic container with a fresh chicken dish with some veg and herbs, he picked that up and also some new potatoes and paid for them quickly at the express till. Back to camp, he went, he got to the field just as it was spitting down with rain. By the time he had got the bike over the barbed wire fence surrounding the copse and over to the tent, it was pouring and he was soaked. He managed to get his fire started and cooked his meal first boiling the potatoes and then the chicken. He put some olive oil over his spuds and with the chicken next to it sat back in his tent and enjoyed his meal. The new potatoes were lovely and made the whole meal tasty; whilst he ate he boiled water and made a cup of tea; he was no cook, but it was impossible to spoil it, he thought.

He settled down for the evening listening to a play on the radio and then listened to the news, nothing new again.

Adrian had put his wet clothes into his dirty washing bag, he needed to sort out his clothes; he didn't have many t-shirts and shorts left, well not much of anything really, so he needed to get them washed. He knew there would be a launderette in the town somewhere and would have to find it. Also he needed to sort himself out in that he needed to trim his beard and moustache and trim his eyebrows; he did that with his shaving kit and looked a bit fresher. He slept well that night, but he also could badly do with a haircut.

# Chapter 23

Adrian was awake early and taking his bike across the field, he cycled to the site of the car boot sale, paid to get in; then wandered up and down the rows of sellers. He managed to buy a fork, spade and rake and hoped that would be ok. He couldn't mow grass of course unless the owner of the house had a mower he could use; he kept up his search of anything at the car boot that he could use, but there was nothing else.

Whilst at the boot sale, he had asked a couple of sellers where the launderette was and had been given an address. He tied the things he had bought to his bike and went to the launderette. He put his clothes in the wash and dried them in the tumble drier. He cycled back to his camp and settled down. It was early afternoon; it was his intention to get back out fishing and catch some supper.

He went quickly to his fishing spot and sorted out his fishing gear; it was well into the evening when at last he caught his dinner, a mackerel, and put it in his bag. He pulled out some seaweed and put that in his bag as well, then he went for a quick swim, towelled himself dry and walked back to camp. Whilst he was walking, he picked up some foraging items for the pot, nettles, and dandelions. The whole plant was both edible and tasty, as were the nettles. When he got back to camp, he washed the nettles and dandelions well and then put them in a billy to cook. He had a few potatoes left so he cooked them first; removing them, he cooked the dandelions and nettles. Cooking in his other billy was the fish which he had filleted and added a drop of oil and seaweed. He enjoyed his meal which he ate in the dark as night had fallen. He had made a fence of shrubbery around his camp to shield the light from his fire from passers-by; he made a cup of tea, and it was ok but he had to use powdered milk as he had run out of proper milk.

That night, he had a phone call; it made him jump as he had forgotten all about it. John Hogarth was the person who had rung for some garden work to be done, he asked for an address and was glad that it was local. John asked him for a couple of hours; he tried to sound business like and said that he had a cancellation for 2:00 pm the next day and it was agreed that he would be there to work. He would have to sort out payment but would do that tomorrow.

He slept well that evening and woke up to a beautiful sunrise, washed and dressed, he went along the lane near his camp and looking out, found some mushrooms. He picked a handful; they would be nice for dinner. He returned home got on his bike and made it into Lymington. He went to a local barber and had his hair cut and feeling better, he went back to camp and made a cup of coffee with powdered milk. It was while he was enjoying his cup of coffee that the phone rang. It was his first customer asking him to come round and take a look at they're garden. Adrian said that he would get there that afternoon, and then had to scramble to find the pen and paper to take down the address.

The afternoon soon came and he cycled with his gardening tools to the address that he had been given by John Hogarth. The grass was long and there were plenty of weeds and that was just the front garden. He rang the doorbell and after a while, it was answered by an older gentleman with a walking stick.

The man asked him in, and they discussed what was wanted. The man said that he needed the front garden done first, he had an electric lawn mower doing nothing in the shed and would be more than pleased if Adrian could use that. The front garden was the priority; then the garden needed edging and weeding. Adrian explained that it would probably take longer than two hours to edge and weed it and that he could only accept cash as he had lost faith in banks.

All was sorted and he started getting the lawnmower out of a shed at the bottom of the garden. He mowed the lawn after adjusting the settings to a few inches. He explained that if he did a final cut on it, it would leave the grass yellow and straggly. There was an edging tool in the shed, he put down a string line and cut the edges nicely. He next used a hoe to start removing the weeds; he had been busy for 90 minutes now and the owner, John, brought him out a cup of tea and some biscuits. He hadn't enjoyed a biscuit for ages; it was great and he enjoyed it. He carried on working and finished 10 minutes late and whilst he was packing his tools away, John chatted to him. It was obvious that the gentleman wanted company and gardening was just a part of it. He didn't mind that, he had nothing else to do. And it was nice to chat to someone.

John paid him and asked if he could come every week; he said that he could if John could afford it. He asked if Adrian could do the back garden. He explained that he understood there was a lot to do in the back and asked him if he could do a full day's work at the weekend to get the garden into a manageable condition. Adrian agreed to start that weekend if the weather was ok.

The days were passing slowly with still no change in the news, and it was getting to him, and as it was Wednesday, he would go and try to catch a fish; the same place as ever.

The weekend dawned overcast but dry, he was back round to John's Garden, he went into the shed and got out the lawnmower and tools.

He cut the lawn as he had in the front garden John, as before brought him out a cup of tea and biscuits which he enjoyed.

"Would you like me to put a chair outside for you?"

"Yes, please if you could."

Adrian then edged the lawn, then pruned the roses and other shrubs and then weeded the beds. He talked and chatted away whilst he was working. At the end of the day, he took the chair back in and John paid him; he cycled back to his tent. He put all the money he earned in a tin and dug a hole to put the tin in, pushing a piece of turf on it to keep it concealed. He thought about moving abroad and how he would get a passport; he needed an address to send it to. Knowing the way some of these departments worked, he didn't think that his application would be notified to the police, so hopefully they would still be unaware of his whereabouts.

# Chapter 24

It was necessary to steer her people the way that she wanted from looking at Adrian to looking at Ronnie Tyler.

"Right, people, listen up," said Jean.

"We now need to concentrate completely on our new suspect. We believe that he may well have come into the country on a forged passport. We know his real name, but not the one he is using now. And we don't know if he lives locally or not, but he has been seen twice in the Norbury area. We currently have no picture of him. So, I want some of you to try to get a picture and that would include from Australia."

\*\*\*\*\*\*\*\*\*\*\*\*\*\*\*\*\*\*\*\*

He had several phone calls to ask him to do gardens locally and before very long, he had a little list of regular clients.

Although he wasn't due to visit John for a few weeks, he knew he could just drop by for a cup of tea occasionally. He was thirsty now, so he got his bike back out of the field and cycled to the supermarket where he bought a pint of milk, a readymade meal he could cook on his fire, some more apples-

Coxs this time as there were no Russets, some chocolate and a cake.

On returning to his camp, he lit his fire and made himself a cup of tea with milk. He sat on his sleeping bag and enjoyed his tea and cake. This was the start of his new life. He would resume his gardening the next day. He had to get back to reality, so he was intending to relax tonight; some while later, he started cooking and sat there eating his dinner with the radio on but now, he could just chill out playing music, he finished off with an apple, and then a bit later, the chocolate. He went to sleep and woke up to a clear sky and a pleasant temperature. He made tea on his fire, some of the wood had become embers and he managed to stoke the fire to boil water. He went first to the supermarket where he bought a tin of curried beef and a bag of basmati rice. He had his dinner for later; it got nearly to 2:00 pm, he rode his bike over to John Hogarth's Bungalow, parked his bike in the front garden, unpacked his garden tools and went to the front door. John answered and smiled at him. "Ok to start?" Adrian asked and yes was the reply. He took his equipment round the back and John opened the back door and handed him the key to the shed.

"Are you coming out?" He asked. "I'll bring your chair out if you wish, it's a lovely day again."

"Yes," John said, "that would be good."

Adrian brought John's chair out. Then taking out the lawnmower, he lowered the setting down to the lowest they would go; he mowed the back garden.

It looked good; "John beckoned to him to join him in a cup of tea. He sat down on the grassnext to Johns chair, I feel that I must be honest and tell you of the problems that I have at present." Adrian went on to tell John about his arrest; in fact, he told him everything.

John said.

"Have you been living in a little tent all the time whilst you are here?"

"Yea," he said, "it is quite comfortable. There is something I would like to ask you," and explained to him about the passport.

"I don't need it now, in fact, until the arrest thing is sorted. I don't intend to leave the country any time soon, but I need to go see a few places and decide what I want to both do and where I want to be."

"Could be still in England, but as I say, I'm not going for a long time, so don't worry, your gardening isn't at risk. I don't need it till all this arrest thing is sorted, I'm not after fleeing the country," he repeated.

"Ok," John said, "I've been thinking about things too, firstly, it is fine for you to use this address for your passport, but also, you are still camping, and the weather is becoming increasingly wetter and colder. I have a proposition for you. How about this, that you move in here with me? As far as rent is concerned, the whole place needs redecorating, making it easier and nicer for me in my final years. I'd still pay you for the gardening, but you do the redecorating for free, you can still do your gardening jobs for whoever you want."

Adrian was amazed to be offered a roof over his head by someone who didn't really know him and would spend time with him in a house on their own. The house was in urgent need of decorating, so he could see that John would get a lot out of the arrangement.

It didn't take much for him to agree to that, but he had to think of John and tried to think of some way that he could give him some security but could think of none. He would just have to work his socks off.

John then told him that he had an old van in a garage on the side of his bungalow, he hadn't used it for a while, but if Adrian wanted to use it, then he could, on buying tax and insurance and getting an MOT for it. He understood that Adrian didn't want to pay through a bank, but he would do it for him if Adrian paid him. Adrian unlocked the garage and had a peek at the van; it wasn't too rusty, so he decided to get it sorted.

He agreed to move in straight away the next day.

# Chapter 25

Adrian woke up in the morning and put things into the kit bag and checked the garden tools strapping on the bike.

He rode down to the bungalow and knocked on the door. It was answered by John, and he went in. John showed him the room he would be staying in. They sat down to a cup of tea and just chatted. Adrian told John what he had planned for himself and how he intended to get on the property ladder eventually and his employment. He explained how this murder of a very dear friend had catapulted him into the situation he found himself in now.

John was impressed with the optimism and stoicism of Adrian, how he had worked out a future for himself and wished him all the luck in the future.

They talked about the renovation of the bungalow, John had said that he wanted to do it well but economically; Adrian knew that this meant as cheaply as possible which was fine.

They decided to look at the whole project, to sort out the largest and most complex task. They realised that the most expensive would be the kitchen which needed new appliances all over except for the fridge freezer as that was new. The largest job would be the removal of the wall between the kitchen and dining room, it definitely needed removal as the dining room was hardly used, Adrian had checked that it wasn't a supporting wall so that wasn't a problem, so the first job was to remove the furniture from the dining room and spread it around the bungalow then mask everything up to ensure that dust didn't penetrate everywhere. Then he could start knocking it down, the skip was in place and he had found an old door in the garage that he could wedge onto the skip to run the wheelbarrow up it and tip stuff in. The lounge needed redecorating but apart from it, that was ok.

To keep the cost down, he needed to get John the cheapest price; to do this, he needed to get hold of a computer so that he could buy online. It would be back to the postcards again, making an advertisement that a laptop pc was wanted.

He had a phone call that same evening from a lady who had a laptop for sale and didn't want too much for it, so he paid for it on collection after seeing it working.

He slept well on a comfortable soft bed that night and the next morning he sat with John who was in his dressing gown and had a cup of tea and some cornflakes. Then he cleared the table and started to move the furniture about, the table went into the lounge, some chairs went into his bedroom and a sideboard also went into the lounge. He ripped up the carpet and then started removing anything on the wall which was going to come down; that done he sat down with John who hadn't been able to do much, and had a cup of tea and biscuits. He found a large club hammer in the shed and he went at demolishing the wall with gusto and with a few knocks, had smashed through the stud work and demolished the wall quite easily transporting it by wheelbarrow out of the house and into the skip.

He then checked the van out quickly and put the battery on charge; he hoped that he could then start it but expected it to need a new battery; then it was on his bike with empty kit bag to the supermarket. He bought some items for their dinner spuds, greens, gravy granules, an apple pie, custard, mustard and horseradish sauce, he bought a couple of bottles of lager and returned home; well, it was home now. He had been in John's fridge freezer and cupboards and couldn't believe how he had been living and eating. He could soon alter that with some decent meals. Sunday, they did nothing, it was a nice day so they had the windows open and sat chatting; in between, he boiled the potatoes, then put them in the oven with a beef joint he had bought locally and roasted them. When the beef was nearly ready, he put the greens on and boiled them and used the water for the gravy mix, then plated up and they both sat and enjoyed it with a pint of larger each. For pudding, they had apple pie with some tinned custard. They both had a nap in the afternoon sitting in their chairs, it was a good start and they both realised that him moving in was for the better for both of them. Adrian had the benefit of having a proper roof over his head and a nice comfortable bed to sleep on. On the other hand, John had the benefit of an able-bodied companion to keep him company and help with the things that he was unable to do.

# Chapter 26

As soon as Jean arrived in the office, she was called over by Jane Dores. "I think that our escaper has surfaced at last, but not quite where we thought he was, he's fitted himself in with a local man in a village, it was only a local copper who recognised something about him and after a little thought realised who it was, shall we bring him in? He is doing gardening jobs around the area. Apparently, he's moved in with an elderly man."

Jean thought for a moment, the papers and public think that we are still after him, then came to a decision. "No, let him be for now, tell the local bobby to watch him without alarming him. We have other irons in the fire and whilst he is still being searched for is giving us cover for the things I am planning."

She thought for a while then called Jane over, "Right, I've decided what we should do. I want him to keep away, but we need to keep him on our side about it, so we need to talk to him. We can't afford anything to interfere with things now. Fancy a little trip out?"

They used Jean's car as she didn't want to use a police car and drove down to the New Forest, stopping for a cup of tea at Burley. He's picked a nice place, its beautiful down here.

They got back in the car and drove to the address that she had for him.

They quietly went to the front door, but on listening they heard voices around the back; walking around they found him sitting chatting with an older man who was in his seventies at least. They were sitting in rattan chairs with a table.

"Good afternoon," Jean said, "I'm sorry to startle you."

Andrew was a little shocked and tensed up then relaxed. "Okay," he said, "you've found me."

The older man said. "Is this the lady, you told me about?"

He nodded.

"We're not here to take you back," she said, "only to ask you to maintain a low profile. We do have other investigations going on and your return could well interfere with them, so all we are asking is that you keep quiet, and don't come back until these investigations are finished. Let me just stress, this is in your own best interest. This could well be in your favour, so that's all I ask. Is that ok?"

"Yes," he said, "received and understood."

"Right!" she said, "we will be off then."

"You can turn your phone back on now but don't use it to contact anyone to do with the case such as walkers. And don't answer it if they ring you."

He walked with them round to their car.

"Thank you," he said.

They got in and drove off.

*******************

Adrian sat quietly for some time in his bedroom, this was a positive move but after so long being the only suspect, it took some getting used to; it meant that he could plan for the future. However, it wasn't definite that he was off the hook; things might change again, but going on the run again did not appeal to him at all. He would just have to wait and see what happened.

The next day in the evening, Andrew started to remove the old wallpaper in John's dining room with good results. He found that by soaking the wallpaper in one area about a metre at a time; then he went to another wall and soaked the same size area, then back to the first and soaked it again, then back again to the other area and the same then back to the first and using a cheap scraper he had bought at the supermarket scraped off the old wallpaper. It took a couple of days to remove it completely and prepare the wall for re-papering. He had removed the wall between dining room and the kitchen. It had been a stud wall so the damage to the other walls was slight and just needed some plasterwork in places. He bought some plaster to patch where he needed it.

He looked online with John at kitchen units, second-hand ones or whatever, some had hardly been used and looked pretty good, so it was John's choice and he eventually decided on a kitchen set up and they went for it buying it online and arranging that Adrian would pay on collection so that he could check on condition. It was still installed in another property at present but would be taken down carefully by the next day; one reason for getting it was that it wasn't too far away to collect. The van had proved to be ok and after checking the oil and tyre pressures and fitting a new battery, he had got it through the MOT, he paid John who paid for the tax and for him to be insured on it.

Having the van meant that he was able to collect it, he was pleased when he got there as the cabinets which were of course still put together fitted easily into the van and whilst there, he bought the sink and even the cooker from the same vendor, so it would also fit and didn't cost too much. The vedor helped him load it into the van and back he went and unloaded the van and put all the kitchen parts in the dining room. In between working at the bungalow, he answered his phone a few times and had several more appointments for gardening. Things were looking up at last.

He and John were getting on well. John was telling him about his working life, he and been a pipe fitter and welder using steel or stainless steel from 1 inch to 24 inches in diameter, where he built pipelines for steam, welding each section together. John told him about the things they used to get up to at work, having a laugh. They got the work done but in between, they were all guilty of some practical jokes on each other.

He went to bed late and woke in the morning and went out and spent several hours smashing everything in the skip flat to leave plenty of room, as the cost of hiring the skip was so expensive.

# Chapter 27

**Melbourne, Australia**

Ronnie Tyler arrived off the boat with his wife Elizabeth, who was ten years his senior; they moved into a house in a fashionable part of Melbourne; the neighbours heard them rowing often.

It was alleged that whilst Ronnie Tyler was known to chase other women, he would stalk his wife making certain that she could form no contact with others around her. She was not allowed to go out to work, or out anywhere, he, on the other hand, could do what he wished and when he wished, and how often. He was a prolific gambler, and within a few years, he had gambled most of their money away. The rows grew worse, he had never worked, and the money had been her inheritance. One day he had returned home driving an old motorhome. He had told the neighbours that he and his wife were going to tour the country for a bit. The motorhome set off early in the morning. The neighbours had grown worried for the wife whom they never saw and didn't answer her door to anyone, they had called the police several times. The police had visited, and his wife had answered the door, and told them that there was no problem, so they had no cause to do anything. The property was left unoccupied; the police later had a question of her whereabouts from a relative in England who couldn't get through to her by phone, so there was a missing person's report that the police were acting on and the first thing they did was force entry to the house. It had been 3 months before the Police search had started. Ronnie had a very good start on them.

......................

She had been fast asleep in bed when he got in.

He had pointed the 22 pistol at the back of her head and from a distance of a foot pulled the trigger three times; the pistol had been fitted with a silencer as it hardly made a sound and so no one had heard it.

This was a callous murder with no thought for her at all, a truly horrendous crime. He wrapped her body in the sheets that she had been sleeping in. He had the motorhome outside and in the early hours, he took the body and dumped it in the back. He closed the doors and drove it into the outback on the motorway. He obeyed the speeds and other signage until he reached an empty part and then drove off and drove into the desert; the ground was hard so there was no problem with getting bogged down and stuck. He took out a fork and shovel, using the fork to loosen up the sandy soil, he used the shovel to make the hole. When he had finished, he took her body out and buried it.

The police searched the property and finding nothing of consequence sent in their forensic team.

The forensic team found a considerable amount of blood when using special lighting which made the blood illuminate as the blood had been cleaned up; they were looking at a murder investigation. The police looked urgently for the motorhome; it was their suspicion that he had moved the body using it. To be thorough, the forensics had used equipment to look for a concealed body, including specialist dogs and ground penetrating radar with no results around the property. They investigated his friends and discovered that he was involved with dodgy characters who dealt with drugs, and almost anything he had probably met them in connection with his gambling.

The motorhome had vanished off the face of the earth with no trace.

That was the state of the investigation in Australia, and it was still ongoing.

Knocking door to door, they had found a couple of witnesses who had seen the body being moved to the van, or what they thought could be a body.

Checking what cameras they could, they found one at a petrol station which still had archives they could access and so found the direction of travel; they knew that the motorhome had not reached the next town as the road had been closed because of an accident 20 miles from Melbourne and no traffic had passed beyond that point. They used dogs trained to find bodies; they looked initially for tyre marks off of the motorway and followed them till they stopped. they were fortunate that there was little rain so tyre marks still showed up. They let the dogs out and were rewarded quite quickly with both dogs indicating a find; they gave the dogs their treats and then put them back in their cages in the vehicle. They took out shovels and began to dig and after a while, they found the body first the sheet came in sight; they covered it up with a tarpaulin sheet and then called it in on the radio for the team in general and pathologist to attend the site.

The police had put out that they were looking for him, and the motorhome of which they had the number plate.

The police were hopeful that they would find the van eventually, but it would take time. They checked that he had not hired it from a hire company which they found he had, and the company was quite anxious to get it back.

The police checked the areas where they usually turned up and of course, there was a wreck which was burned to a crisp and forensics soon told them that they could find nothing that would help the police find him. But it was the correct camper.

# Chapter 28

It was 12 o'clock and Adrian left in the van to his appointment with a pensioner couple and started work on their garden. He was mowing and cutting for the rest of the day; they supplied him with tea and biscuits and he worked hard. He enjoyed a chat with them afterwards and was happy that they were well pleased with what he had done and made an appointment to visit in a fortnight's time.

He went home feeling happy that his gardening business was off and running well. He got in and had a long shower, then a cup of tea with John, then started work finishing repairing and filling the walls of the now kitchen dining room. He had also removed the linoleum from the kitchen. He turned off the water and took out the sink. John had got a gas fitter to disconnect the cooker, so he just had to remove it and get it into the skip. He had to ask a couple of men walking by to help him lift it over into the skip, which they did without a problem.

As far as decoration was concerned neither Andrew nor John had any idea of a colour scheme, but a friend of John's came round and looked through some pattern books and chose wallpaper, curtains, tiles and worktop.

Adrian started by panelling the floor with clip-together type of wood planks; they were light oak as this would keep the light colour.

He plumbed in ready for the sink to be put in as he re-housed the cupboards in position, so by the end of the next day, he had the floor done and the cupboards installed. He put the new worktop on and cut it out to take the sink and cooker. The cooker and hob would be installed the next day by the electrician; he wasn't using gas. Then he could tile. John had an electrician as a friend, and he had put in the sockets and livened them up.

The next day he had another appointment for a garden; this one was particularly overgrown. He did a first cut on the lawn and that took him most of his time, so he arranged to return the following week as he didn't want the cost to be too high.

That evening, he started tiling, and he made a nice job of it. He took it one step at a time using all the complete tiles, then he put in the tiles that needed cutting. The following day, he grouted them all. And finished the painting.

The following day, he had yet another appointment, it was just weeding, but it was a fair-sized garden, so took some time. He went home with his back aching. Even so, he managed to finish wallpapering the kitchen and dining area.

That evening, he didn't do anything. John and he had been living on takeaways from one place or another. So, it would be nice to have a proper meal; he was able to use the hob and cooker now.

Adrian went shopping and bought the ingredients for a cottage pie. The fridge was back in the kitchen now and the walls were wallpapered in the kitchen area. Adrian with

John's help got the rest of the furniture back in. The table and chairs and the cupboard were all heavy or awkward, and although John had helped, he hadn't helped very much, in fact, he had hindered rather, but Adrian realised that he had to believe that he was helping for his dignity.

# Chapter 29

**Back in the UK with the Police**

The police had a list of the people who had come into the country; they were delving into the carpet clue, but they were getting nowhere. They looked for a link to anyone entering the country and buying carpets but found nothing.

Jean was disappointed. But she knew that her man had been seen twice in Norbury. She called Sergeant Walters to her.

"Right," she said, "we can't find any matching details with carpet sales, but we know he has been seen twice in Norbury. So, let's make use of the cameras in the area, let's examine all of them starting from the centre of Norbury. It will be tedious, and we will need to talk again to Sally Parsons and hope she can find him on tape. We will start with cameras near where she saw him; as soon as he is pointed out, and we have pictures of him, then we can look further. Let's collect the available film before it's deleted. If he was seen in Norbury twice, then it's likely that he is living nearby. So, dates on the films don't matter now, we just need to find him on any film and take the date from that one."

Jean called Sally Parsons and asked her if she would come in again.

She arrived that afternoon.

"Whereabouts was it you saw him, be as specific as possible please?"

She said it was outside Iceland supermarket.

"And the time please as accurate as possible?"

"I was shopping, so it would be about 4:00 pm on Sunday because all the shops were shutting."

"And when else?"

"I really can't remember when else I saw him."

"Ok, thank you, we will get some film for you to look at and hopefully point him out. I'm afraid that it may take some time though."

They took the film that they had managed to obtain from Iceland. They managed to locate the footage about an hour before and thirty minutes after the time that she had specified. Sally looked through the footage but could find no sign of him.

"Disappointing but let's try from another angle, we have some tape from the jewellers opposite which shows the outside on the pavement." They did the same one hour before and 30 minutes after.

Sally went through the tapes again, she was a little refreshed as she had been given coffee and biscuits, and after about an hour, she saw the man she was looking for. It wasn't good footage, a bit bleary but it was something.

Jean thanked her for her time and arranged for a car to take her home.

The rest of the police in the office then looked on their screens for the same figure; they were all looking at film from different cameras at the same times to attempt to see whether they could trace his route passing him from one camera to another; the trouble being that a lot of the film for that date had been written over.

It was soon apparent that although they had a blurry picture of him, that's all they had.

Jean sent the picture to the technical department and hoped they could enhance it.

In the meantime, she had all her staff looking through films of around Iceland at any time to the present and hoped for a result.

DC Niall Glover called her over Jean, "Do you think that this could be him? It looks as if it could be to me."

"Yes, it could be, let's assume that it is, now taking that time, let's work his route out, this was only yesterday, so all the camera footage is fresh." They looked for him on other cameras.

DC Janice Harwell called her over. "He is on here now." Jean went to her desk and opened a picture of the Norbury Area Map on it, then she put the points on it where he was seen.

It carried on a bit till she had two more points but no more.

"Right," she said, "we have a direction, let's use that. We know he lives in this direction. We also know that he didn't travel down the road to pass by Warwick Road, as there's a camera there and he's not on that one, so he must be in between. I want a surveillance car on that route to watch out for him. Thinking about it, we know that the film showed him going away from the town centre, so we can assume that he lives somewhere in that direction, so in which case there must be a film showing him arriving. So if we can find that it will give us an arrival time and we can reverse it so that we can see where he came from."

"That may help us find his house, we have him at the start of the high street, and he is not on any film from Warwick Road Junction. So, he must live somewhere in between. Let's have a look at where we can put the surveillance van where it will not be noticed! Get Sally Parsons back in to make certain that we are watching the correct person, we have better pictures now."

They managed to get the surveillance van on someone's forecourt and after a day wasted, they were in luck and saw him walk down a road a little way from them; they were too far away to get out and see which house he went into, but they now had the road.

The next step was to get the surveillance van parked down the road. This would give them the house where he was staying. They were in luck once again as he popped out to buy some cigarettes. This gave them his house at last.

Jean decided that they would arrest him the next day early in the morning. They would arrest him for the Australian police and not let him know that he was being held for Jennifer's death, as they did not yet have adequate proof at present. As soon as he was arrested, SOCO would be able legally to search his house and hopefully come up with something which would incriminate him.

The next morning, they all met in readiness at the police station and drove out in convoy. Two police cars, one at the front and one at the back and in the middle was a police minibus which was full of minibus seats but only four were being used and next to that was the van, with a secure area in the back with bars, the prison for the fugitive.

The convoy swept through the streets, lights blazing but no blue lights.

Ronnie Tyler had been up early as he was going to Basingstoke to see a mate about money. As the lights from the convoy swept into his road, the lights came to his attention in a mirror and with the lights off, he saw them deploy outside his house. He had enough time to get out of the backdoor and down the back garden and down an alley between two houses, into the road behind. The police who had quickly got into the back garden to cover any attempt to flee, caught a glimpse of him running and gave chase.

One of them radioed through to command who let Jean and the others know what was happening, the police cars rushed around to patrol the adjoining roads, their blue lights flashing. They forced Ronnie to turn round and run back the way he had come, straight into the path of one of the policemen. Ronnie was armed with a knife and was threatening the policeman when he was tackled from behind and brought down; other policemen dived on him, one of them grabbing the knife and in a few seconds, he was handcuffed and restrained whilst the van came round, and they put him inside.

# Chapter 30

He was taken by the van back to Croydon Police Station where he was charged with resisting arrest, carrying an offensive weapon, using a forged passport, and being wanted for murder by Australia. He was taken down to the cells and locked in.

The rest of the team went to breakfast. It was an upbeat meal as Jean had paid for it and they were buoyed up by their success in catching him.

She addressed the team, "Ok, we have our man, but now the work begins, we need to correlate all the evidence against him for the DPP so they can get ready for court."

Jean left him to stew in the cell for a couple of hours then he was brought to an interview room.

In the meantime, his residence was being searched and examined minutely by SOCO; they took samples of carpet, and other surfaces, took swabs of anywhere of interest as well as photos to show the residence and anything they needed to take away; they sprayed areas with luminol to see if there was blood anywhere.

The bad news for the police was that no blood was found, or any matching carpet, and that looked to be all they were going to find when one of the detectives going through paper from the bin found an invoice for renting a garage. Jean looked and said, "I wondered why he was escaping on foot, with no car nearby which could belong to him, let's look at that garage."

When the garage was opened, there was a van inside and it was carpeted in red; SOCO again was called to investigate.

They found some splatters of blood on the roof, very small but enough for the forensics to check the blood and get DNA from it.

The carpet which was new still gave them some other evidence as it also contained a small amount of blood drops, the fact that he had put the red carpet down probably disguised the fact that blood was there, so he hadn't cleaned it up or removed the carpet.

# Chapter 31

Jean started by asking Ronnie Tyler his name and that he was being held by the Australian police as they wished to talk to him about a murder. He first said that he wasn't the person who was wanted. However, they took his fingerprints and DNA. They looked at his passport which they had found in his house. It was a forgery and the only good part of it was the photograph; they already knew his real name from Sally Parsons earlier.

They were now in possession of enough evidence that they could arrest him for the murder of Jennifer; from the evidence, they could see that she had been murdered in the van, and her body taken to Mitcham Common where it was found.

They surmised that he had kidnapped her and tried to have sex with her, but she had not let him; he had lost his temper and hit her with an implement of which they weren't sure, and she had died immediately. The reason her injuries had been to the back of her head was that she had been trying to escape.

The only thing that puzzled them was that her body was found in one place, but the rest of her clothes were found elsewhere.

Jean was disappointed that on a very thorough search of Tyler's house, no sign of the missing jewellery was found. She had hoped that he had kept the jewellery for himself to use to think back on the assault, a sort of memento, and use it to remember his feelings at the time.

Then she thought more about it; there had been signs that Tyler was hiding something from them, and it was giving him immense satisfaction. What could it be? It had to be something that she had not seen as relevant at the time but obviously was.

All the facts they had were put to him, to which he answered 'no comment' to everything.

They took him to the custody sergeant, and he was charged with Jennifer's murder. Jean got all the paperwork together and sent a copy to Inspector Johnston of the Australian Police, then rang him up to explain to him what had happened, he listened and then asked her what they could do to assist, or what would happen now.

Jean wasn't sure as that would be up to the Department of Prosecutions.

They would have to sort out what should happen as there was a murder in two different countries. Later, it was decided that he would only be charged with the murder of Jennifer, that way when and if he ever got out of prison, he could be immediately deported to Australia to face trial there.

Jean had still thought about what it was that Tyler thought he had over them and was also aware that the evidence they had was not absolutely certain to obtain a conviction. What the hell was it? She started getting all the paperwork done, People didn't understand how important some of this was, she was looking at the things that he had on him when caught, as normal they had taken his clothes from him and sent them to forensics. His jewellery, watch and money had been stored, he would not get them back until he was released from prison.

Then it hit her; the jewellery he had been wearing, Two gold chains with a cross, and a St Christopher. They didn't fit his profile. She thought, but could they be the missing jewellery from Jennifer? Jean moved fast and with determination, she rushed down to where the prisoners' possessions were kept and filling out the paperwork, she took the box to a table and opened it slowly and carefully. The jewellery was in a plastic bag; she took a picture of them with her camera, then putting it all back, returned to her desk and put a picture that they had of Jennifer from Adrian's phone but was a good close up, and showed her wearing the chain with the St Christopher and compared it to the one in Tyler's possessions. They matched; she asked Sergeant Walters to send the possessions to forensics because the chain was full of gaps which could contain skin particles and so DNA.

"Yes! I hope this is what you are concealing from us, hiding in our faces; well, we have it now," she said to herself.

He appeared before a court the next day to put in a plea. he was asked how he pleaded and said, "Not Guilty."

He was remanded in custody and sent to prison till his trial which was pencilled in for three months' time.

Detective Constable Isabel Johnstone wondered if there were any other things that could be attributed to his past; she decided to look at cold files of a few years before he had gone to Australia.

As she had expected, there were quite a few crimes at this time, plus she had to go through them all, so it was at this point, she had to get the files and so had to inform Jean and see what she wanted to do about it. Jean looked at her work and told her to run with it and that she would get her transferred to Basingstoke temporarily. That way she could go to the scene of the crimes there and get a feel for them and if our suspect could be responsible for them.

Isabel was given a room in the police house where all the new constables and others were housed, which would save her coming back home each day, she was single; so no problem there.

She went home to pack her clothes for a week but didn't think it would be that long she was away; she was fairly tall about 6 feet tall she had a slight figure and a pretty face with a dark complexion. She wore a minimum of make-up but didn't need it.

Her flat was tidy, neutrally painted with a few ornaments and potted plants, she made herself a cup of tea and sat down kicking her shoes off and resting her feet on a stool. She was going to give it an hour or so before she set off, it would take about ninety minutes to get there.

She took her coat, put her shoes back on and grabbed her case and went to her car which was a little Suzuki. She drove off and following her map went via Guildford, over the hogs back and on till she reached the M3 then straight to Basingstoke. She found Basingstoke Police Station without too many problems and parked around the back so that she was near the police lodging house, and walked over to the station. They were expecting her, so she was shown straight upstairs to a vacant workstation which had been set up for her.

It wasn't till the following day that she sat at the workstation logged in and start going through the files; there were a lot of them that could possibly be down to Ronnie

Tyler. There was no sign of him on the Basingstoke or nearby reading list of offenders.

She began to sort through the unsolved crimes on record, putting in the dates she needed, the computer spewed out a long list.

"Hell," she thought, "this is going to take ages."

But she had to start somewhere; she started by putting in his address whilst in Basingstoke. And then where he went to school, John Hunt of Everest, she went there to talk to any teacher who had been there at the time that both he and Jennifer had been there.

There were a couple that remembered him and they both said the same, amounting to Ronnie Tyler being a bully both demanding and vicious; both teachers were pleased when he finished school. They had no end of complaints about him, but there was nothing they could do at that time.

Isabel went back to the station with written statements from the teachers and continued looking at old unsolved crimes. There were a couple that caught her eye; one was an assault on a young lady of about twenty, Ronnie Tyler had been interviewed about this crime as he fitted the description of the assailant, but the victim had not wanted to carry on with the case and Tyler had just sat with a wicked smirk on his face whilst interviewed. Isabel could well understand it; Jean rang for an update and Isabel told her about things she had found out. Jean was pleased and said for her to carry on looking for anything she could find.

The next thing she found was another assault, she opened the file and was intrigued to find that there had been no one arrested and facing a court hearing, the girl had only just survived and had been bludgeoned about the head. However, she had not been able to identify her attacker as the injuries that she had sustained had left her unable to speak.

She decided to investigate further. The first thing she decided was to go and take a look at where the offence had happened. But that would be tomorrow.

Morning came and Isabel drove to where the attack had happened, or at least where the girl Judith Hass had been found. She was found in Silchester near the well-known Roman Town, Calleva was to be found. She parked in the car park, then walked around to where she was found, by the Roman Walls, they were made predominantly of flint and were 20 feet tall. There was a long-wooded area surrounding it, making it a very secluded place, she had a wander around to get to know a little about the place and get a feeling of the crime.

She was a little while, the actual site was very interesting, she then drove to Judith Hass's home in Popley, Basingstoke. The door was opened by her mother, and she was let in. It was a three-bedroom house and had been adapted to suit Judith as she had lost the use of her legs due to the attack. Isabel explained why she was there and that she would like to talk to Judith if she could. Her mother agreed but wanted to be there as well in case her daughter got upset.

Her mother talked to Isabel about the attack, Judith had been walking around the Roman Town perimeter as she was interested in how the excavation was going. She had been attacked from behind and hit over the head with something to make her pliable to the whims of the attacker. The attacker had ravaged her then hit her again and left her for dead. She had been found by a couple of archaeologists strolling around the pathway surrounding the town before going to bed on the farm at the centre. They had called the police and ambulance and she was rushed to hospital, was in intensive care for a few weeks, they didn't really think that she would survive. The police had found her bag and so her identity and had rushed round to get her mother to the hospital as her survival was very much in doubt.

Judith came into the room; she was in a wheelchair. Isabel asked her whether she could remember the attack; she nodded, she had got some of her memory back but was not fit enough to face court, and it would only open old wounds. Isabel showed her a picture of Ronnie Tyler, she nodded but said again that she could not face court.

Isabel left the house having said that she would contact her boss and see what could be done without her having to go to court.

Isabel returned to the station and rang Jean; she explained the situation that Judith had identified Ronnie Tyler from a photograph. Jean said that she understood that Judith didn't want to go to court, but she said that Isabel should get a written statement from Judith, to make sure that it was signed and witnessed, and then they could use it. and they could make a video of her answering questions, and that might be able to be presented to the court.

Suddenly, it came to her, "When you go back to see her could you take fingerprints and a DNA sample from her, and ask her whether she had any jewellery taken?"

Isabel went back the next day and obtained the samples, and also confirmed that Judith had a cross and chain taken.

Isabel didn't have to do the interview on film; that would be the prosecution department's job as they would be presenting it at court.

*********************

Jean spoke to the prosecution service about the addition of Judith's evidence and that it needed to be filmed and correctly shown in court. They agreed that the filming was their prerogative, that they would sort that out and that Tyler needed to be charged with that offence as well.

But there must be no more mention of the Australian murder as when he had finished serving his sentence in England, he could then be arrested and extradited to face a trial and then prison in Australia. To this, Jean would have to formally remove the arrest by the Australian police.

Jean visited the prison where Tyler was being held on remand and he was escorted to a small room, which contained a table and chairs, which were bolted to the floor so that prisoners could not use them as weapons. Tyler was handcuffed to a prison warder and made to sit down at the table opposite Jean, a tape recorder was set up on the table and Jean again spoke to say who was in attendance the date and time.

Tyler said nothing.

Jean then officially un-arrested him for the Australian police and charged him with:

Murder of Jennifer.

Rape of Judith Hass.

Attempted Murder of Judith Hass.

False imprisonment of Judith Hass and Jennifer Harrow.

Actual body harm of Judith Hass.

Possession of an offensive weapon when arrested.

Asked if he had anything to say, he replied, "No comment."

Jean then told him that evidence in the form of DNA had been found on jewellery belonging to him. The DNA was for both Judith and Jennifer.

His face was a picture of rage.

Jean felt absolutely satisfied in his anguish and had great trouble concealing a smile.

# Chapter 32

John heard all about it on the news and called Adrian as soon as he could. Adrian listened to the news and then caught it on the next edition on the TV, he took the van and drove to Croydon the next morning.

Adrian had a meeting with Jean.

"I feel that I need to apologise for the trauma that you have experienced, and I understand that it will be very difficult to get a good job, but as you decided that it was best for you to abscond and go into hiding, I am afraid that there is no compensation or help coming from the police force to help you."

"I understand what you are saying, and see that there is nothing I can do, as it was my decision to run, but I hope you can understand why I did it."

"Yes, I understand, but not officially."

"Is it completely over now?"

"Sure, it is, may I wish you the best of luck for the future."

"Thank you. Can you tell me where Jennifer was buried, I would like to pay my respects."

"Yes, of course, her mother had her cremated at Basingstoke Crematorium. I'm not sure whereabouts there, but I'm sure they can tell you."

Andrew left the police station, Jean walked him out.

"Goodbye, and good luck."

"Thank you, goodbye."

He returned to the van and drove to where he had lived and came away with some clothing and other bits and pieces he had left there, that took him only a few minutes as his stuff was already put in a corner of a downstairs room. He went from there to his old firm to collect his tools. He went in and was greeted by some of the blokes working there; he collected his tools then after saying fond goodbyes, he drove down to Basingstoke, and found directions for the crematorium. He drove into the car park and went to the office where he asked where Jennifer was interred; a girl behind one of the desks showed him. He had brought some flowers and arranged them on a circular epitaph with her name on it, he sat down and talked to her as if she was there, and told her what had happened, and how he felt about what had happened to her.

He drove back to the bungalow; he was hungry so taking some mincemeat from the fridge, he made John and himself a Spaghetti Bolognese. He had purchased some fresh bread and a couple of bottles of St Miguel on his travels, so he sat and watched TV with John. The news came on and the arrest of Ronnie Tyler and the innocence of Adrian was shown with pictures. There was a little background to the murder investigation given then onto the next item.

He rang Mrs James to let her know that he was back from an urgent call home and would be round to sort her garden out again.

Mrs James was not happy with him and said on the phone that he was no longer welcome as he had been arrested by the police and even went on to demand that he pay her money back over the time he had been working for her.

He could not believe it, but as she started to shout down the phone at him, he switched the phone off; it took him a while to get over that call but decided that she was a one-off and he rang other clients and explained, "I have just got back from Croydon where I had been arrested, I was accused of murder. I can assure you that I am not guilty. I have been released by police now and wish to continue with your garden work if that's ok?" It was to his dismay that the other women that he gardened for were all known to each other. They had the same opinion of him and didn't want his gardening know-how again. Oh well, he thought he would write out new postcards with his old phone number. He went to sleep a bit troubled as he would probably need to move on. It would postpone his thoughts of the future. He would move on to Dorset and set his camp up; this time he could use his bike and that meant that he could move a good distance quickly. He lay there on his bed that Dorset had a fair amount of elderly people that may need help with their gardens.

******************

It was good to get that part of the decorating done, next would be the lounge but he had another appointment the next day. This wasn't too bad, just mowing and edging the grass which wasn't too long, so he gave it a good cut and then edged it as well making another appointment for a fortnight's time.

They moved the furniture three-piece suit into the dining area and started stripping the walls. John had asked that they put in French windows they looked online in the adverts using a web site that advertised second-hand stuff, and sure enough one came up. They were only able to get some as they were not encumbered by size because they had not made an opening for it, they would make the hole to size.

Andrew was worried about making the hole, so they paid a builder to do it, he put in a lintel and then knocked out the wall. But Andrew wheelbarrowed the rubble into the skip to save a small amount.

The next day, he managed to get the French windows into position and then plastered the corners neatly using concrete on the outside but plaster on the inside. Again, the wallpaper had been picked for them and it didn't take very long to finish the room and using the same planking that was used in the other rooms on the floor, and he managed to get the furniture in.

The next morning, John wasn't feeling very well, Adrian had an appointment but said he would drop into the chemist on the way back and get some of the cold relief that John preferred. He took the van and went to visit the old couple whose garden he had started a couple of weeks before and gave their lawn a shorter cut and weeded, he was given tea and biscuits.

He chatted for a while, and it was decided that he would work there once every fortnight.

On his way back, he dropped into the chemist and bought the medicine. On his return, he found John still unwell and made him some chicken soup which might help. "Ok, let's see how you are in the morning and if you are no better, then I will ring for the doctor." He went to bed early as well as he felt tired out.

The next morning, he woke early and went to check on John; he seemed worse, so he rang the doctor, who thought he ought to get a Covid test kit, for himself as well. He took the van to the chemist and returned with two lateral flow tests, he was ok. John's, however, was positive; thank goodness, it wasn't positive for him as well. It meant that he would have to keep an eye on John and if he deteriorated any more then he would ring 999. As he was working mainly for pensioners, he thought it prudent to stop working near them. He gave them the choice of him turning up to work without coming into contact with them they could either pay him by leaving the money somewhere or leave it till his next visit, He said that they shouldn't leave refreshments for him as anything he touched needed to be disinfected.

He got back on the phone and talked to the receptionist at the doctor's and explained the situation. John, it seemed was getting worse. A little while later, he took a cup of tea to him and he was far worse and he called an ambulance, they came wearing all their protective gear, and took him to the hospital. He was warned that he would have to be quarantined for ten days, so work was out of the question. He rang his clients and warned them that he would not visit them for two weeks as he did not want any risk of them catching it. They understood as did nearly everyone in the civilised world.

There was nothing he could do now; there were a few things to do in the bungalow, which he did then sat down with a cup of tea and watched the telly. He couldn't even visit John as visitors weren't allowed.

The phone rang the next morning, it was the hospital and they had bad news, John had passed during the night. He had his wallet on him and he had a card in it as he had a prearranged funeral they would take his body and the ashes would be interred in their gardens. They asked if he could sort out the registration of death at the registrar. He wasn't sure what he needed to do there but the hospital had some paperwork for him. He would need to find John's birth certificate. He looked through some of John's paperwork and found his birth certificate and marriage certificate. He took them and the hospital paperwork to the registrar, where they gave him some burial certificates and other paperwork. That was it, as far as he was concerned, it was all done. Even visiting the registrar was weird as he had to wear a mask and do everything through a Perspex screen. When asked, he asked for five copies of the death certificate.

He couldn't face doing anything that day, he just thought about how John had been to him; it felt odd he couldn't do anything but stay in the bungalow.

It had all changed, he had just gotten used to having a future and now he didn't.

The post arrived as normal the next day, there was a brown envelope which was addressed to him it was his passport, at least he had something else to think about now.

A couple of days later, there was more post and amongst them was one addressed to him. On opening it, he saw that it was from a local solicitor, asking him to make an appointment. He guessed that they would be asking him to leave, but how long would they give him, he hoped to get a couple of weeks. He explained that as he was in isolation, he couldn't attend for fourteen days, the receptionist said that was fine and made him an appointment for close to the end of his confinement.

Adrian went to his appointment with trepidation, and on being shown into a room with a large desk in it and some chairs opposite it, he was given a chair and some coffee. The Solicitor Mr Tiffin introduced himself as acting for John, he explained that John had made a will. "I must read it out as it is Mr Hogarth's wish." Mr Tiffin could see that Adrian was looking worried and smiled and said, "In short, Mr Hogarth, has left everything to you, the bungalow, the van and everything." The solicitor said that Andrew must have come to mean a lot to John and that there were no relatives. It would take a while for the estate and money to get to him but he would get it as soon as possible. There was a considerable amount of money in the bank about ten thousand pounds, so he would get that too.

He came out of the solicitors in a bit of a dream he went for a long walk eventually ending up back at the old campsite where he sat and thought things out; he had lost another friend, but this friend had left him financially independent.

He had nothing to do the next morning, so he took his fishing gear in the van and went fishing at his favourite spot.

He sat there and thought through how his life had changed and most of it down to John. They hadn't been friends for long, but John had backed him one hundred per cent and he really appreciated that, he owed John a lot and he would always know that, but he had to now think of his future. There was no real reason for him to go abroad straight away; he could leave it for a while and stay put, finish off the decorating, get himself a dog and sit pretty for a while. He was feeling lonely and looking back he had for a while, so he decided to see about getting a dog. He didn't want a puppy;

he would get one from a rescue centre. He would have to look where the centres were.

All of a sudden, he had a bite and striking quickly, he had it on the line; it fought him back and it was a long time before he brought it in, it was a cod about two pounds in weight. He dispatched it quickly and gutted it, then cut off the tail and head throwing them back in the sea. He put it in his bag and made his way back to his van. He drove back to the bungalow and took his catch into the kitchen, he cut the cod up and put three pieces into the freezer. He would have the other bits later. He made some batter up and some chips; he started cooking his chips and halfway started cooking his cod fillet then whilst they were cooking, he buttered some bread and took out some tartar sauce, he plated it and enjoyed it.

# Chapter 33

He had to decide what he was going to do next with his life. It had been his intention to move to warmer climes and he was still investigating the opportunities. There were quite a few, he wanted a large place he could both live in and use as a hotel so that he could be there and run it after first doing it up from nothing. His first thing to do was get the bungalow valued to find out how much it was worth. That would give him a value for his total worth.

Should he keep gardening and make a living doing that at least until the guy that was under arrest in Croydon was put up for a trial and he could go to court to watch? It sounded a bit callous, in some ways but he was curious, as it could have been him up there.

The decision had really been made for him by John; he was in a bungalow, and he had funds in the bank, so he did not have to rush into anything he could just stay put, earn some money, and enjoy life.

He had been looking at the postcards in shop windows to see what was going and one advert was for someone to take over the ownership of a Labrador of three years old. The dog although well trained in walking and basic training had caused the owner a lot of money and hassle by ripping the place apart.

He knew that Labradors and Retrievers would do this, they just got lonely, this wasn't a problem for him as he intended to take the dog with him when he was working, so he rang the number and arranged to go over and see it. The dog needed to be gone in a very short time, he got the impression that this was the dog's last chance. He just wanted a friendly dog who he could love and would learn to love him, it would also have to be soppy with kids and anyone as he was going to take it working with him, he wasn't looking for a guard dog.

The dog greeted him fondly; she was a black Labrador, *good start*, he thought, and talked to the owners. They hadn't realised what a bind a dog could be, taking them out for walks and feeding them on time, they suddenly found that their lives weren't their own anymore. Even so, they kept the dog outside in the back garden, so it wasn't really a pet at all.

He wasn't worried whether it was male or female and it hadn't said on the postcard they wanted forty pounds for her.

It felt wrong to barter for her, so he just paid, and led her out by her lead. She walked with him willingly and he had no problem getting her into the van and onto the front seat, where he put the seat belt on her, she looked puzzled at that but was fine. He drove home talking to her as he drove, "Well, Sheba, it's nice to have you with me. This can be the start of both of our lives if we get on together. First things first, I need to get you some food and then we can go home. Then it's off to work tomorrow and you are going with me." The next day he took her with him to his first job which was a regular gardening job for pensioners whom he had become a regular worker for, he asked if it was ok to bring Sheba in with him whilst he was working, and they agreed, and Sheba took to them straight away especially when she was bribed by them with a biscuit.

The date of the trial came up and Jean received a visitor, Inspector Johnston of the Australian Federal Police had arrived to see the trial.

"Nice to meet you," he said to Jean.

"And you," she said.

"You've come to watch our legal system in action, have you?"

"Yes," he said, "should be fun."

She said that they should go out for a cup of coffee before we go to the court which is of course The Old Bailley.

On entering the Old Bailey Jean, Sergeant Dick Walters and Inspector Johnston were seated behind the prosecution counsel.

Jean glanced up to the public gallery and saw that Adrian was sitting there. She wasn't surprised; she would have done the same in his position, she would have been there in his position. Also present were Jennifer Hewitts Mother and with her was Judith Hass's Mother.

The court itself was oak panelled, in fact all the furniture was oak and gave an instant picture of officialdom interspersed with solemn standing. It gave the impression of severity, an appearance to make the guilty quake. It didn't do a lot for the innocent either, but it was obvious to all that it was a place without much humour where things were done efficiently and somewhat ruthlessly.

The court stood up for the judge to take his place, and then an usher asked Ronnie Tyler his name and address.

He continued, "You stand accused of murdering Jennifer Harrow how do you plead?"

"Not guilty," he replied.

You are also charged with the Assault and rape of Judith Hass.

He pleaded not guilty to that charge too. There were a few minor charges to which he pleaded not guilty too as well.

The prosecution stood up and gave a quick presentation of the facts and how they were going to prove them.

After the deposition, the Defendant, Ronnie Tyler called his defence lawyer over and they whispered to each other for a couple of minutes then the Defence Lawyer stood up and said that his client, Mr Tyler wanted to change his plea to guilty.

The Judge asked Ronnie Tyler if this was correct to which he replied that it was and the Trial was over, the judge said that he would hear mitigation tomorrow and would sentence him then.

He then adjourned the court until the next day.

The next day dawned, and the court was brought back to order. The judge came in and sat down.

The defence lawyer started his speech saying that Mr Tyler had pleaded guilty to help the court save some time, and that he was sorry for the crimes.

The judge was silent for a small time, then stood up. Ronald Tyler, you are a callous and merciless murderer You display no remorse for the crimes that you are guilty of and the public ned protection from you, so I sentence you to Life Imprisonment and to serve a sentence of no less than thirty years. I further sentence you for the other offences to ten years and that to run concurrently. Tyler showed no emotion as he was led away by the warders, he never even looked up.

Jean and her little party were well pleased with the sentence and even more when Mrs Hewitt thanked them for the work that they had done.

On return to Croydon Police Station Jean called all her team together and thanked them for their work. It was a disappointment that the trial had been shortened with the guilty verdict, as it meant that the teams hard work would go unheard. However, the sentence was greeted with joy.

The only thing that had disappointed not only Jean but everyone connected to the murder and rape was that the Defendant Tyler, had made no eye contact with any of them, he just couldn't face them.

Inspector Johnston however had more to do and say. He made arrangements to visit Tyler in prison and asked that Jean accompany him.

They went to the prison by car and were escorted to a room and Tyler was brought in, Inspector Johnston Immediately told him that he was being indited for the Murder in Australia and would be hopefully extradited to face that charge as well.

He would then if found guilty would have to serve both sentences, both in Australia and in the UK. He said nothing.

Johnston took Jean to the White Bear pub where he was staying and they chatted about the cases and relaxed. He had to return home the next day and was more than happy with the way things had turned out.

Milton Keynes UK
Ingram Content Group UK Ltd.
UKHW020617281123
433366UK00014B/293

9 781035 838776